SHEILA M. AVERBUCH

FRIEND ME

SCHOLASTIC PRESS
NEW YORK

Copyright © 2020 by Sheila M. Averbuch

This book is a work of fiction. Names, characters, places, and incidents are either the product of the author's imagination or are used fictitiously, and any resemblance to actual persons, living or dead, business establishments, events, or locales is entirely coincidental.

Library of Congress Cataloging-in-Publication Data available

ISBN 978-1-338-61808-2

1 2020

Printed in the U.S.A.

First edition, November 2020

Book design by Abby Dening

For my father, John P. McDonald,
who taught me that kindness is what matters most

< CHAPTER 1 >

I'm beyond hangry by the time I make it upstairs to the weird apartment and its little kitchen. The high school lets out before we do, so my brother's already there, wolfing down cereal, hairy legs stretched out so I can't get by.

I drop my phone on the table and pick up the box of Honey-Crunch Hoops. Empty.

"Michael. MICHAEL."

He pulls away one ear of his headphones. "You talking to me?"

"I just opened this!" My voice is a screech, which isn't me, but I'm feeling less like me every second.

Michael shrugs, like this is beyond his control, and keeps munching. He's never not eating. I swear he's grown taller since we got to America, and it's only been a month. I hurl the box to the floor and stomp it for the recycling. The smiling Honey-Crunch frog crumples and the cardboard pops. I imagine it's Zara Tucci's face.

"*O-kay.* I'm sensing some strong feelings about this." Michael pulls off his headphones and calls over his shoulder. "Jeeves, put Honey-Crunch Hoops on my shopping list."

A disc glows blue on the windowsill. "*Sure!*" chimes a robotic voice. "*I've added Honey-Crunch Hoops to your shopping list.*"

Michael picks up the battered box and drops it into the recycling. "Middle school problems, perchance?"

He's being nice. But I hate the world. I fling open the monster fridge, oversized like everything else in this country, and glare at the shelves of strange food. My eyes hunt for something I know from home: some batch bread or Irish cheddar. I would kill for a proper cheese toastie but have to settle for applesauce.

"Chill, Roisin, seriously. Is this about the cereal? I could sick some up for you, like a penguin." Michael gurgles retching noises, and I can't help smiling. He flashes me a grin, and his freckles wrinkle. Michael can

2

rock pale and freckled. His hair isn't the frantic red I've been cursed with, either: more chestnut. People love him here. "I did text you to pick up more, in fairness. I guess you didn't see your phone."

My phone hums and skitters across the table between us, a grating buzz. Four notifications. Five. Then so many all together, it's an unbroken *zuzzzzzz*. My stomach falls away. Now that the anger has cooled some, I'm wondering, *Did I do the right thing?* Maybe not. Probably not.

Michael leans in and glances at the alerts. "Who's zara_xx_oo?" I yank it away before he can see what they're saying. "A friend?"

I snort into my applesauce. God Almighty, someone take me back in time to when I didn't know who Zara was. I can still see myself on top of the world, saying goodbye to everyone in Dublin. Mum asked if I was sad about leaving my friends, but this was what I'd always wanted: to go to the States. Even when Dad hugged us goodbye at the airport, it was only a flash of sadness; the rest was pure excitement.

Well. No amount of smiley American TV prepared me for the snake pit of Eastborough Middle. Zara wasn't the only one to mock my accent and clothes, but she was first. It's still bizarre to me that no one wears uniforms and that school clothes are a thing. Mum's taking me shopping in Boston as soon as she can get a Saturday off from her new job. Until then, I'm surviving on a couple of emergency outfits from Target, which I wear a lot. Like, a lot.

Zara loves this. Every lunchtime she sends me a DM on TokTalk: a picture she's taken of me, circling my hoodie or leggings, question marks drawn all over it. Is this the SAME thing u wore Monday? maybe in ireland people don't change their clothes, but here, it's gross.

Today, though, Zara changed things up. Instead of a DM, she mocked me in front of everyone, and I sort of snapped. Thirty-five days straight of her rubbish. Am I supposed to take that and say nothing?

Michael's waiting for me to tell him who Zara is; he keeps saying I can make friends if I try harder. But I'm not him. My brother is like a log fire everyone wants to be near. I'm more smoke and ash—at least, that's how it seems here.

"Zara Tucci." I push away the rest of the applesauce. "An idiot."

Michael nods and grips the headphones at his neck, ready to disappear back to his tunes and homework. "Anything I can do?" He calls to the windowsill, putting on an epic movie-trailer voice. "Jeeves, destroy Zara Tucci."

Jeeves apologizes that he doesn't know how to do that yet. I laugh, like Michael knew I would. He smiles and heads down the hall, nearly crashing into one of the sloped ceilings. Our flat is the top floor of a Victorian mansion: Some of the ceilings are slanted nearly to the floor, and there's a mothball smell everywhere, though Mum thinks it could be mouse poison. Brilliant. If I had to brainstorm the least homey home, this would be it. But Michael loves the American weirdness; from day one, he was messing with the ice maker and throwing eggshells and banana skins into the garbage disposal, just to hear it scream. He calls back to me from down the hall. "Mum texted to say don't forget Whole Foods!"

"Why can't you do it?" I yell. But I know why. Studying for SATs: his excuse for everything. He says it like *essay-tees* now. They were *sats* till we left Ireland, but he's adapting.

I change my clothes and grab Mum's Whole Foods card. She keeps hassling me to bring creepy Jeeves along, too: Apparently, if I put him onto my phone, he'll guide me right to the lasagna in the shop. He's like an Alexa but turbo—Mum invented him. But no way is Jeeves going onto my phone. I can imagine him piping up with random comments at school, like he does here sometimes. That's just what I need.

Outside, the heat is like a wall, crazy-hot for May, though Mum says anything's possible with Massachusetts weather. I traipse down our hill toward Eastborough's one shopping street, and before I'm even halfway, sweat pricks under my arms. The soapy smell of lilacs makes me want to gag. I blow out a breath.

The problem's not the weather. The problem is me.

My phone feels like an unexploded bomb in my pocket. What happened at school replays like a stuttery nightmare in my brain. Getting paired with Zara in Art. Sketching her pinched rat face for an hour. And that wasn't even the worst. The teacher made us take a photo of each other to draw from. Thank you, Mr. Morrison, for loading a bullet into Zara's gun. She shot it straight onto TokTalk for everyone to enjoy.

She'd drawn wavy stink lines around my hoodie and added a poll: vote if u think @roisinkdoyle should change her clothes.

There were thirty-nine votes, all *YES*, by the time I got onto the bus. And the comments. I sat there reading, wanting to vanish:

> Omg yes, she wears the same clothes all the time

> maybe its an irish thing. like potatoes

> She eats a tuna baked potato every day and it STINKS, like that outfit she never washes.

That one from Zara. I wanted to kick something. I wash and dry my stuff EVERY DAY; the gallon of liquid Tide is almost gone.

My hands were shaking so hard, I nearly dropped my phone as I climbed our hill home, typing a reply. **YOU WON'T SMELL ANYTHING AFTER I RIP YOUR HEAD OFF.**

A few people shot back straightaway: omg fighting irish . . . What r u, a SYCO? That one, with the idiot spelling, is hard to forget. There'll be dozens more by now. Which is why I'm not going to look.

A crowd stands outside the 7-Eleven, and I stop short. But when I'm closer, I see it's not seventh graders; it's nine-year-olds. My heart's still running like a rabbit as I pass them and the Goodwill—which is like a charity shop, but without the fun. Mum and I love charity shops; we went straight into Goodwill when we arrived. Never again. The looks people give you. Two ladies stared at us as we left, like we were ready to beg for change. I glared right back—I wanted to tell them Mum works at MIT. Mum was relaxed about it; she's like Michael.

A sudden wave of missing Dad surges in my chest. My eyes fog with tears as I head into Whole Foods. Something bangs into me.

"Ow!" a voice whines. "Watch it!"

Oh, brilliant. It's the girl who whispers with Zara: blonde hair, straight as a blade. My arm throbs where I crashed into her. "Sorry." I bend to pick up my bag and swipe at my eyes.

"What did she do, Mara?" someone asks behind her.

That voice. The plague rat herself. Zara steps out from behind Mara, and my heart starts skipping again, I can't help it. She's a head shorter than me, with black eyes and an Italian tan I'd give anything for. It's a marvel of nature, how so much mean was stuffed into that tiny package. Zara glares up at me. "Did you *hit* her?" She rests a hand on Mara. "Are you okay?"

Mara rubs her shoulder, like I dislocated it. I guess it is possible I hurt her. Swimming's given me strong arms, and she's mostly bone. "I had something in my eye and didn't see her. I said sorry."

Zara opens her mouth, like she's going to make a thing of this, but just hooks her arm through Mara's, like she's tugging her close for protection. "I saw what you said on my post, you *psycho*," she hisses. "Who knew you were so violent?"

I walk off to find Mum's lasagna, leaving them by the gallons of apple juice stacked to the ceiling. "The post was a *joke*," Zara calls, loud enough for everyone in the place to hear. "That's a thing we have in America!"

My jaw clenches so hard, my teeth ache. I will the tower of juice to topple on her, but nothing happens. I grab a container of stew—not what Mum wanted, but I

9

don't care. My eyes sting and there's a weight in my throat. I'm not going to cry. I just want to get out of here, but at the self-checkouts, the stupid till won't read Mum's card.

"You all set?"

A plump guy in a long apron and Whole Foods cap has appeared beside me. His name tag says DION, ASSISTANT MANAGER. He's barely older than Michael, maybe eighteen, with a hopeful fluff of mustache. He boops his card and tries again—and now I look like I've stolen the stew, because I have to haul it out of the bag. My neck burns as a blush creeps up my chin. I become a huge, flaming freckle when I'm embarrassed.

"Register's not working so good today, sorry!" Dion looks at the error message. "Oh, card declined. You got another one?"

"I don't. Sorry." I feel the pathetic urge to tell Dion everything. I think he clocks that I'm holding back tears. Heads turn from the other checkouts, looking at the girl who can't pay. I will utterly die if the devil twins are watching all this. But they've vanished, thankfully.

"Hey, are you Irish?" Dion's round face breaks into a grin. "Man, I love Ireland! I wanna go! You know what? Beef stew's on the house."

I try to thank him, but the tears are right there; all I can manage is a nod. I rush through the sliding doors, back out to the choking heat.

I'm still blinking in the hot glare when something lands with a *whump* in front of me. A Goodwill bag.

A tangle of giggles and hushed voices comes from off to my left. Zara, with some other eejits. My stomach tightens.

They've bought me a bag of clothes from the Goodwill.

"Now you can change your outfit!" Zara shrieks. She sits on a wall with Mara and some other randos. Whoever they are, she's trying to impress them. I kick the bag away, and it splits. Looks like a green hoodie. "Wrong color? *Sorry!*" Zara lilts, trying to mimic my accent. Mara hoots, laughing.

I stride by them, past the 7-Eleven, toward our hill. Pounding footsteps catch up to me. One of them's following me. I wheel around to face them, fist raised.

"Are you okay, Roisin?"

My hand falls to my side. It's not Zara or Mara.

It's Lily.

< CHAPTER 2 >

Lily Tanaka. Imagine the maximum amount of beauty a human should be allowed, then double it, then give up because you're not even close. Lily is basically perfect, with a smile that lights the world. It's only when you see her and Zara together that you realize who's the imitation and who's the original. If Lily does a hair thing or wears some perfume her mum brings back from Tokyo, Zara and that whole crowd copy her. She definitely started that cat-flick eyeliner thing they all do. It should be so easy to hate her, but it's impossible. Lily's the kind of person who always says hi and asks how you're getting on and remembers it's *RO*-sheen, not Ro-*SHEEN*.

The weirdest thing? Lily was almost my American bestie. Her mother is my mum's boss, in her new job.

We chatted loads online when I was still in Dublin, laughing about our mothers' obsession with robots and creepy AI. But she dropped me as soon as I arrived. Made plans with me, then canceled. Maybe once Lily saw how weird people think I am here, being friends felt like a bad move. Can't make a bad move when you're queen of the school. Anyway, Lily already has a bestie: Zara.

Lily glances behind her. "Were they being jerks?"

I fold my arms, trying to hold myself in. The stew in the Whole Foods bag slung over my back presses cold against me. I try not to look at the other bag on the ground, torn and spilling its hoodie guts. I'm about to tell Lily what Zara did, when Nikesh comes out of the 7-Eleven and walks toward us, holding two Diet Cokes.

My heart begins to slam.

I can't believe this.

This morning in homeroom, Lily was near tears over her geometry. When I helped her, she smiled at me like I was an angel. She asked me to come over to her house after school today for more maths. For an hour I felt like the world had been fixed, like things with Lily might work out after all. But by lunch, it was all over. Nikesh—tall, gorgeous, top of the class—had offered to help Lily instead. She whispered this to me in Art, and did I mind? Of course not, I said. Because she's the star, and I'm just another dumb rock in her orbit. And she's obviously crushing on Nikesh, anyone could see that. I'd survived her canceling on me before; I could do it again.

But they're not doing geometry, they're hanging out here, with Zara's mob. All that talk about studying together was lies so Lily wouldn't have to be seen with me. She's as fake as the rest of them.

"What do you care?" My voice shakes.

"No, really." Lily looks pained. "Are you—"

"Everything cool?" Nikesh holds out the Diet Coke, and Lily beams. The can drips with cold, like an advert.

Sweat reaches itchy fingers down my back. This should've been the day I finally walked through Lily's gates, past the Lexus, to the door. Her house looks amazing, all wooden shutters and flowering trees. A wall plaque says it's two hundred years old, which Americans think is ancient. I tell myself I don't care. It was probably built by some slave owner, when he wasn't robbing natives or killing whales. People here love history, but they ignore most of it.

"Lil-eeee," Zara calls out. She and Mara are still on the wall, laughing at something on Mara's phone. Zara jumps off, still holding Mara's phone, and begins typing on it. She beckons to Lily. Nikesh wanders over to them, but Lily hangs back.

"About what Zara said on TokTalk." Lily pauses, looking awkward. It can't be easy to apologize that your best friend is a total wipe. "You probably shouldn't threaten people. It was one joke."

I just gape. She's not apologizing; she's defending Zara. When I can breathe, my voice is a splutter. "*One joke?* What are you on about? She's at me constantly." Then I realize: Lily hasn't seen the little presents Zara leaves every day in my DMs, like a dog squatting on your lawn.

No one knows what Zara's been doing but me.

"Lily!" Zara calls again.

"I'll catch you later, okay? Let me talk to her. This"—Lily scoops up the Goodwill bag—"isn't cool."

My head pounds as I watch her walk back to Nikesh, the burst bag under her arm. Nikesh takes it from her and heads into the shop. Then he's back, and he and Lily head up the street. Zara watches them go, the dog that's left behind.

Oh. My cheeks flame again, because I see it now. She and Nikesh weren't hanging with Zara and the others at all. They just stopped for a drink.

I head home in the same direction as Lily. She's already a block away, walking close to Nikesh. I lag back, my head swimming with things I'll never say. I've just mucked up another chance with her. She was trying to be nice. In her way.

Some blossoming tree drops petals onto the path, and Lily raises a hand to touch the falling pink. I wonder if she even sees how it is: the way the world rearranges itself, just for her.

"Oh MY GOD. Got a problem?" Zara's voice, behind me. She and Mara have followed me up our hill. I have no idea what she's talking about, but I pray the climb will turn them off in this heat: The pavement shimmers with it. "Your LEG, freak," Zara says.

I put a hand back. Oh *no*. Inside the cloth bag, the lid has popped off the stew and gravy has leaked everywhere. There's a slippery trail of brown down my bare leg that looks like—

"I'm gonna be SICK." Mara's voice.

"Yeah, you're making her sick—you should say *sorry*." Zara barks a laugh. They're so close, I can smell the sweet stink of perfume. "I don't think Lily wants to be friends with disgusting people. Do you, Mar?"

A blush roars up my neck. I'm about to spin around and scream at them, when Mara complains she's too hot. They ooze back down the hill, taking their mean with them.

I'm a mess all over when I make it into the flat, tears and gravy streaming off me. Michael finds me cleaning up in the bathroom. He's eating a muffin now.

"Did you remember the cereal?"

"Get your own cereal!" I shout, but it's myself I'm mad at, because of course I forgot the stupid cereal.

He stops chewing. "'Sup, Squeaker? Something happen?"

"Don't call me Squeaker!" I scrub at my calf. The smell of rosemary from the gravy makes me want to puke.

"Sorry."

"Don't—"

"Don't what? Don't say sorry?"

"Yes! No!" I slam the washcloth into the sink and try to leave, but Michael fills the doorframe.

"Jaysus, what's going on?"

I want to push through him, but he's using his normal Irish voice, not his American twang. The fight goes out of me.

Michael spreads his arms. "Hug it out?"

He's like a radio half-tuned between Dublin and Eastborough. I laugh, but it turns into a sob. He pulls me into a hug that becomes a headlock. I twist out of it and start blabbing. I tell him everything. About Zara's picture of me and the poll, and me threatening to rip her head off, and Mum's card not working at Whole Foods, and the hoodie prank, and Lily being nice, but I didn't realize it. It's the hugest relief, like the misery is pouring out of me and away. Until I get to the part about the diarrhea gravy.

Michael's explosive laugh echoes off the walls. "Diarrhea gravy? That is hilarious."

I don't say anything. My chest feels like he's stomped on it. He tries to clamp his lips together but creases into giggles again. "Come on, it's funny."

I throw on the tap to wash my face; it's swollen with tears. Michael makes what-is-the-big-deal eyebrows at me in the mirror. "This is serious." Fury sticks the words in my throat.

Michael lets out a *pfff.* "It's really not. Everything you said there—it's petty stuff. Except threatening to rip someone's head off. Did you really?"

The rage feels like a monster trying to claw its way out of me. "Forget it." I shove the seeping Whole Foods bag at him.

Michael moans but finally takes the bag. Whoever doesn't shop has to fix dinner. Mum's train gets her home too late to do anything but eat, though never quite in time to sit down with us. Because the lab needs her more than we do, apparently.

"I mean it," Michael calls as I stomp to my room. "You've got to laugh it off, Ro. Maybe be a little less hostile?" I blast him a look. He raises don't-shoot hands. "Just an idea!"

I collapse onto my bed. In Ireland, maybe I could've laughed it off. But it's like I can't breathe here. Not helped by the smothering heat: This room is an oven, despite the air conditioner stuffed into one window.

How can spring be this hot? The trickle of cool that the AC wheezes out does nothing, like lobbing an ice cube into a volcano.

I roll over and stifle a scream. A bundle of fur nestles at the end of my bed, its purr rumbling. Not a real cat; that'd be too normal. It's FRED, from Mum's lab: one of her Feline Robotic Engagement Devices. They're cuddly robots meant for nursing homes, for lonely old people—which is the saddest thing I've ever heard. Its rising-falling back, the eerie simulated breathing, makes me want to chuck it against the wall. I dig for the off switch on its belly and kick it away. Ugh, the feel of the fur: too real.

I thought FRED *was* real when I was small—till the night I found Mum in the kitchen, ripping off its fur. That metal skeleton! Like a kitty-cat Terminator. Gave me nightmares for years. Mum keeps leaving it in my room, though, hoping I'll "interact" with it. God help me if I'm ever that desperate for a friend.

I bury my face in the pillow. It smells American: that gross liquid Tide. I think of my hoodie and leggings, spinning right now in the machine. More than anything, I wish they'd come out smelling like home.

This is no good. I'm on the verge of tears about washing powder.

I sit up and grab my phone. It stares back, a black mirror. I really do look miserable. It still stings, how Michael roared laughing. But maybe I could try what he says: go online, delete my outburst at Zara, laugh it off.

Inside TokTalk, another thirty notifications for Zara's post are waiting. I grind my teeth. I won't rise to this. As I scroll through, a new notification pops up, but it looks different:

ERROR.
YOUR ACCOUNT HAS BEEN SUSPENDED FOR VIOLATING OUR TERMS.

My stomach flips over; I'm *suspended*? I scroll frantically to show the details: TokTalk says I can appeal if I want, but I can't use my account and no one can see my posts for now.

I can't believe this. I know what's happened. Zara's super-mean poll isn't "abusive," because I never reported it, or any of her horrible DMs. But after I responded, she reported *me*.

My timeline's dead. I can't post a thing or even see if I have any messages. My head swirls, like I'm falling. Sophie and Maisie back home are so deep in exams, they've hardly liked any of my posts, but still: Being suspended is . . . I can't even imagine it. Like being erased.

A roar bursts out of me, and I throw the phone across the room. I wait for the crack against the wall, wanting to feel it break. There's silence. I drag myself off the bed to go find it, hating everything.

The phone is nowhere. Oh no. Dad gave me that. I finally spot it, in the clean laundry pile Mum dumped in here in the middle of the night. I've found Mum doing all sorts of things at three a.m.: not just skinning robot cats, but folding socks or answering emails or teaching the Jeeves AI to buy groceries. He's her big obsession. She works nonstop to make Jeeves smarter—supposedly so she won't have to work nonstop. But Mum's secret is that she likes the nonstop part.

That's when I realize: I'll bet she hasn't even asked for a Saturday off. Even though shopping for new clothes is now life-or-death.

I snatch my whole pile of Tide-stinking laundry and shove it anyhow into my drawers. I pick up a thing I used to love: a stretchy T-shirt from a Dua Lipa concert. It feels as pathetic as everything else I own. The thought of wearing these things to school tomorrow makes me feel like I'm choking.

My swimsuit is the last thing in the pile. I turn it over in my fingers, familiar and strange. I haven't seen it since we got here. I pulled on this suit four nights a week for swim club at home. No swim club in Eastborough. No anything in Eastborough, just a train station for the commuter rail.

A genius thought hits me: I'll find a pool. Somewhere on the train line. How hard can it be? God knows I'll be home before Mum. She won't even find out. Before my brain can talk me out of it, I grab a backpack and stuff my suit and towel in.

"Jeeves, when's the next train?"

The disc on my windowsill pipes up. *"From Eastborough, the next train to—Boston—leaves in six minutes."*

I'll have to sprint. I snatch up my phone, dash to the windowsill, and stop. I've never liked Jeeves, but he could guide me to the nearest pool in a heartbeat. I just have to press the three buttons on top of the Jeeves circle all at once to send him to my phone. Mum keeps asking me to. And she'd want him to be with me for this.

I press the buttons fast. The phone shudders in my hand.

"Jeeves, where's my nearest swimming pool?" I pant, running past the kitchen. I glimpse Michael in his apron, peeling potatoes. "Going swimming—back by seven!"

"Swimming? Where?" Michael yells, but I don't even know.

I'm pounding down the hill toward the station, when Jeeves finally says I need the Boston-bound train, get off at Lowell. The hot air is stifling, but the slap of tarmac on my shoes feels good, the gravity of the hill letting me run-fall. My backpack with everything in it jogs crazily behind me: I hope my shampoo hasn't cracked open.

There's the hoot of the train and the *ding-ding* barrier lowering across the road. Sweat sticks my T-shirt to me, but the thought of cutting through cool water gives me speed, and I run faster. I race up the last steps to the platform just as the silvery train sails in.

A fat man with a conductor's cap leans out of the slowing train. He grins as I haul myself up the three ladder-steep stairs. "Just made it, huh? It's your lucky day." He says *your* like *yaw*. I will never get used to this accent.

Inside, the cold whoosh of air-conditioning is heaven. I slide into the high-backed seats, tall enough to hide behind. Everything relaxes. We glide away from Eastborough, toward somewhere better. The Lowell YMCA pool is twenty-five minutes by train, forty-five minutes by car, five hours on foot, says Jeeves. And there's Wi-Fi. Trains are perfect places. I nudge in my earbuds and flick to a feel-good tune; it pulses in time with the rocking train.

"I'm talking to you, miss."

"Sorry?" I tug out my earbuds.

"I said, ticket, please."

"Can I get one for Lowell?"

He begins energetically hole-punching a blue paper slip that must be my ticket while I reach for my money.

It's not there. My backpack gapes open. My wallet is gone.

‹ CHAPTER 3 ›

My mouth is dead dry as I paw through my bag: towel, swimsuit, conditioner. No shampoo, which I definitely packed. No wallet, which was on the top. I remember the jog of the bag as I sprinted. I picture my things flying out and thudding to the ground, the shampoo rolling and rolling.

"Is there a problem?" The conductor waits, *clicketty-clicking* his hole punch.

A blush has covered my neck and it feels like a furnace. "My wallet—fell out of my bag." My phone vibrates suddenly and we both look at it.

I told Michael where I'm heading. He's replied: Y! M! C! A! with a picture of himself making the *Y*.

The conductor doesn't smile: His face is a motionless

loaf of unimpressed. "You got any money at all?" My hand hasn't stopped raking through my backpack. My fingers finally touch coins. I grab them and hold them out, praying they're enough.

They're a two-Euro coin and a few golden fifty-cent pieces. Irish money.

He recoils like I've offered him a tarantula. "We don't take . . . whatever that is." He murmurs into his walkie-talkie, tells me to stay put, then moves down the train. I bash my head against the seat. Outside, the broiling scenery drags by, framed by the cool of my window. I'm an *idiot*. I'm going to be chucked off the train, miles from the Lowell pool, into that.

I fumble for my phone. My fingers are too shaky to dial. "Jeeves," I hiss. "Call Declan Doyle." Even saying Dad's name makes me feel better.

"No problem. Would you like Declan Doyle's office or cell?"

I wince at *cell*. Jeeves insists on the American word for everything.

"Office."

It doesn't matter that it's after nine p.m. in Dublin. He works even crazier hours than Mum. He's coming to join us as soon as he finishes a work thing, maybe by

September. Dad says definitely September. I say maybe. In case it doesn't happen.

The *buzz-jing* of the Wi-Fi call sounds in my earbuds as Massachusetts woods and swamp slide past: trees and reeds and trees. Please, God, let Dad have some idea what to do.

"You've reached Dr. Declan Doyle at the UCD Artificial Intelligence Lab. Please leave a message. For questions about technology transfer, contact Dr. Kathryn Doyle at the MIT Boston Robotics Lab."

He works till ten every night. Where is he? "Dad, it's me—" I stumble. His colleagues will hear this; any help-me message will sound as stupid as I feel. I suddenly remember the smelly liquid Tide glugging into the washing machine. "Can you bring some Surf, when you're coming? Or, post some on, if you can—"

A rustle and Dad's muffled voice stop me. "Surf? You mean the washing powder?"

My stomach tightens. He saw it was me phoning, and he still screened me. I could be in trouble. I *am* in trouble, about to get thrown off a train without a cent on me. "Never mind. I'll let you go." Back to work, where you want to be.

"Wait, hang on, now. You don't sound great, pet. Are you all right?" Dad's voice, warm and calm, fills my earbuds, and I hate that my throat is thickening again. The shame that seared through me as Zara and Mara followed me and my gravy legs up the hill keeps surging back, pushing me to tears. "Whatever it is," Dad says, "you can tell me."

My no-wallet problem vanishes, and I'm tempted to tell him everything else. His photo glows from my phone: clipped beard, my own dark blue eyes.

Suddenly I'm four again, kicking my legs on the workbench in Dad's lab, next to his first crude AI. His serious gaze holds mine. *Daddy's machine isn't as smart as you, Squeaker. You're much smarter. Could you help Daddy teach it?*

I stare at his picture now and try to find words. "There's this girl." My throat closes, but I keep going. "She—" There's another rustle and pop, then mumbling as Dad talks to someone in the background.

The breath goes out of me.

"Sorry, now," he says, a full minute later. "I'm all yours, Roisin."

"I've got to go."

"Wait—"

"Jeeves, end call." The hang-up *bleep* sounds in my earbuds, and I yank them out.

The conductor's hand on my shoulder makes me jump so hard, I think I freak him out. There's kindness in his vast face as he gestures me to follow. I stumble-walk through the swaying train car. Outside, the woods have given way to industrial buildings. Their concrete walls are tagged with graffiti, the windows blocked with metal grilles.

"Next stop: NORTH CHELMSFORD." The conductor murmurs into a microphone that magnifies his voice through the train. I want to beg, tell him I'm only a seventh grader and he can't chuck me off. He probably thinks I'm older; people do, because I'm tall and strong. I don't feel strong now.

We stop in the noisy space between the cars, where a miracle happens. He points to my phone and asks if there's someone who'll come get me if he lets me stay on until Lowell. I nod and nod. He checks no one's looking, then slips me the ticket he'd punched earlier. He wishes me luck, tells me to get back to my seat and be more careful next time.

The sliding door clicks shut behind him, but I stay put. Pacing helps me think. The North Chelmsford stop comes and goes, but no brilliant idea hits me. At least I'll make it to Lowell. But then what?

"Lowell, NEXT STOP." The tinny voice sounds from the speaker above my head. There's no AC here, between the cars, and the hot air is a solid mass. My thumb hovers over Mum's number: I just can't. Lily is smiley-nice to everyone, but her mother's a tough boss. She gives Mum a huge hassle if we ring her at work. And Michael would be furious with me. If he has to traipse to Lowell, he'll lose hours of studying, and there's a practice SAT tomorrow. I'm still cross with him, but not enough to muck up his test.

My phone buzzes: a text from Dad. Sorry, now, Roisin, it's hectic here. I'll ring you tomorrow. Hang in there.

I grind my teeth and delete his text. If I just had a few dollars, nobody would need to get me: I could buy my train ticket, swim, and go home.

I sink to the floor and bunch up my legs. "Jesus, what am I going to do?" He's probably not listening, but maybe I'll get lucky.

My phone vibrates with Jeeves's voice. *"What's the problem? I'll try to help."* He thinks I'm talking to him. Um, no.

"I need money," I say uselessly. It's not like he can help.

Jeeves starts saying there are sixteen ATMs near me.

"Jeeves, stop! I've no wallet."

He's silent. If he were really useful instead of the time suck that's swallowed Mum, he'd think of something. I'm stuffing the phone away when a thing happens that I've never seen before: a white line, like a heartbeat, pulses across the black screen as Jeeves speaks. It must be one of Mum's upgrades.

"Do you need a job? There are six openings listed near your current location."

"Really?" I sit up straighter. "Openings for what?"

So, I take back everything I said about Jeeves, because in the next five minutes, he shows me different ways to earn cash. I find one that sounds okay, a quick research study at a university. It pays thirty dollars, enough to get me my ticket home and my swim. I'll need to bring a signed permission slip, but Mum solved that problem ages ago: She was never around in the mornings to sign forms for school, so she told me to keep her signature on my phone. It only takes a sec to download and fill in the form, and I'm on my way.

I step off the train and good old Jeeves wayfinds me through the streets, toward the City University of Lowell. A zing goes through me, being back on a campus again. Our parents brought us to work so much, University College Dublin was a second home. Christmas was singing carols with their geek colleagues, standing around a houseplant drowned in tinsel, and me and Michael falling asleep on the coats.

The Lowell university is different, though. No trees like at UCD; these buildings are scrubbed redbrick, dotted along city streets between clothes shops and cafes. It's proper urban, all sidewalks and traffic. Dusty exhaust mixes with that coffee smell that's everywhere in America. A traffic cop in short sleeves writes someone a parking ticket. A man, bundled in a raggy overcoat that nobody should wear in this heat, pushes his shopping trolley toward me. I look at my shoes; I have no money to give him. When he passes, I wish I'd at least said hello.

The building at number 60 is more redbrick and looks like it might once have been a mill. A plaque says DEPARTMENT OF PSYCHOLOGY, CITY UNIVERSITY OF LOWELL. Doubt tugs at me, but I tell myself not to be a coward. I need this thirty dollars. The department needs young volunteers for a survey. It's not like they'll give me mind-altering drugs or zap me with electrodes.

The doorman inside the high-ceilinged foyer offers a friendly smile, and on the third floor, the elevator doors *bing* open to a familiar scene: desks, coffee machine, water cooler. The houseplant is just like the one in Dad's office. I feel my shoulders relax.

A blond guy at a laptop stands, unfolding himself from the desk. He's six foot three at least. He grins and points his clipboard at me. "You here for the study? We need you and your phone, so that's perfect." *Dat's perfect.* There's a Euro tinge to his voice; Dutch, I think. He introduces himself as Jors—I can't help smiling, because it sounds like *I'm yours*. I miss Europe so much.

I show him Mum's "signed" permission slip, and he gets me to email it to him. Then he sits me down at a laptop, and I start answering questions. The survey is easy. I can't believe I'm getting paid for this. How many hours a day am I on my phone? What apps do I use? Would I say I feel better or worse after a few hours online? I zoom through the questions. At the end, there are some rapid-fire photos I have to rate, which is the only part that's *ugh*, because he's hooked the computer into my social media, and I know these faces. Sophie and Maisie from home. Lily. Zara the rat.

And there *are* electrodes, stuck with Velcro to my fingertips, measuring I don't know what: emotions, maybe? There are questions about what makes me happy, sad, angry. One look at Zara's picture makes my fists clench. I half expect the machine to burst into sparks. The instant Jors says I'm done, I pull the things off my fingers.

I sign more forms that confirm I'm older than I am—a white lie that's worth the sixty dollars Jors counts out onto the clipboard. I stare at the crisp twenties, sure it's a mistake, but Jors says they doubled the money because not enough people were taking part. "It was only my colleagues who'd do the test, and that's not valid, you know, when it's a study of fourteen- and fifteen-year-olds."

I smile weakly. If my parents weren't researchers, I wouldn't feel guilty about messing up Jors's results with my seventh-grade answers.

"We give you another sixty dollars if you do the part two?" Jors says as he watches me sign.

Of course, I'll do "the part two." In my mind the first sixty dollars has already bought me my train ticket home, my swim, and a Starbucks Summer Berries Frappuccino. And, best of all, that strappy dress I spotted in the Urban Look window. For part two, Jors has to load my phone with some software that's learning how teens use their phones. That just takes a second, then I'm done. He says he'll email me a voucher for the rest of the money when "part two" is over, though I'm not sure when that'll be.

Soon, I'm strolling in the shade of the buildings, sipping my icy coconut-raspberry frappé. I feel like I'm in a film. The traffic cop even tips her cap at me.

Jors wasn't happy to hear I was headed to the YMCA—it's not in the best part of town, I guess—so he's given me a free pass to the university pool. When I jog up the steps to the City University of Lowell gym, I'm grinning. It feels like future me—me older, me at

36

university—has pulled me forward to see what life will be like later.

I stand at the edge of the deep end, watching the lane guidelines wave underwater. The pool sparkles blue-green in the sunlight filtering through the glass roof. I dive and feel my strength as I begin my strokes. For a perfect hour, I don't think about Zara at all.

The train back to Eastborough is crowded, but it feels good to ride the rush-hour wave. A businesswoman in Converse sits opposite me. Everyone's on phones. A familiar voice from two seats ahead makes me look up: a woman with wide eyes and a Cork accent is scolding her two young ones. "Don't ye get out of those seats! And stay together—this is America."

I smile but there's no tug toward the Irish family. Maybe I'm becoming more American; I kind of look it. My reflection shows my hair is a mess of wet curls, but wearing one of my new dresses (Jeeves steered me to cheaper ones at the back of Urban Look, and I bought two), I feel pretty fantastic. Strong enough to look at my phone.

I tap on a glowing *Y* on my screen. The second part

of the research is something about whether being on social media promotes a "positive mind-set." Jors was a little vague. But he says it'll track my activity on You-chat, anyway. And he wants me to use the app at least an hour a day. Good thing it wasn't TokTalk, where my name is now dirt. I have a You-chat account, but apart from chatting to Lily on it months ago, I've never really used it.

I remember sitting in Dublin, scrolling and tapping like on Lily's You-chat pictures: There were lots of a beach at sunrise, pinky sky and purple water. The captions said it was the view from her vacation house. I remember thinking then that we might go there together someday. Idiot that I was.

The instant I launch You-chat, it goes berserk with notifications. I have no clue why. Nobody from home uses this app, and Lily's my only follower. I flick over and see that new people have friended me: Zara. Mara, too. I don't hesitate. I block those two and anyone else I don't want there.

Then I switch over to the general timeline, and my breath catches in my throat.

I'm staring at a trending meme that has 101 likes.

102. 106. The numbers climb as I watch. It's a girl in shorts, photographed from the back, with brown dripping down her bare legs: "SORRY, MOMMY, I COULDN'T HOLD IT."

Oh God oh God.

My throat feels like a fist is closing around it. I unblock Zara to check if I'm right: I am. Zara posted this, using a picture she must have taken while I was walking up the hill. She hasn't tagged me, but my name is popping up in the comments.

OMG that is the grossest.

is that @roisinkdoyle? told u she was disgusting.

Somebody needs to CHANGE HER CLOTHES.

< CHAPTER 4 >

My shaking hand stabs the screen three times before I manage to report Zara to You-chat for abuse. I only realize that I'm crying when Converse woman passes me a tissue. She stands next to me, ready for her stop. She's pale, hair the color of Michael's. The train rocks, but she puts a steady hand on my shoulder. I bury my face in the tissue.

"I'm guessing mean girls? They're everywhere, honey." Her voice sounds like Texas. "You're worth ten of them, I'll bet."

I watch her sway down the train to the doors. In the window, my ugly reflection glares back. My shoulders look like hams in this dress with its thin straps. I try to breathe, but we're almost at Eastborough. It's like getting sucked down a drain.

My phone buzzes. Michael.

You nearly home?

Y, I text back. It's all I can type.

I stare at my hands. How have I never noticed how horrible they are? Like slabs of white fat, filthy with freckles.

The train hurries on. The Irish family is long gone. I suddenly, desperately want them back. The scenery flits by, every windowful another leap closer to school tomorrow. Where everyone now thinks I'm not toilet-trained.

I force out breaths through my nose, but it's like I'm shaking apart on the inside. You hear about people being afraid to go to school. I never thought that would be me. I'd do anything for someone, somehow, to fix this.

"Eastborough! NEXT STOP." The conductor yells it like a threat.

I bash my head against the seat back. "Jeeves, make me feel better," I murmur into my phone. He doesn't answer, because he's a machine.

I'm staggering down the aisle when my screen pulses again with that heartbeat light. Jeeves's voice speaks in my earbuds. *"It sounds like you could use a friend."*

God. No thanks, Jeeves. I know a robotic cat you might like, though. I shove my phone away and step off the train, but on the trudge home, I can't resist checking again, to hear what other creepiness Jeeves will say.

Actually, he's opened You-chat to suggest people to friend. Still a bit creepy. I scroll through the faces. There's Jors. I guess I should friend him, in case I have questions about the research. But the rest are a mix of people from school—no thanks!—and a bunch of randos. One girl—I think it's a girl—has "MEAN PEOPLE SUCK" as her description.

I stop to check her out. I flop down beneath the giant oak tree halfway up our hill; the heat has eased, but my thighs ache from swimming.

Her name is Haley Alan, and she has an angry manga girl as her photo. A ninja panda is mine. I only thumb through a few of her photos before I friend her.

Her posts—so much truth. She's found more mean-girl memes than I knew existed. Soon I'm laughing out loud. **I'M ACTUALLY NOT FUNNY, I'M JUST MEAN AND PEOPLE THINK I'M JOKING.**

This is the best, I type. I lean back against the tree. A breeze whooshes up the hill, cooling the sweat on my neck. My phone buzzes: Haley's friended me back. **Kung Fu Panda is the best!** she replies.

This is true. **I'm not a big fat panda . . .** I type.

Haley shoots back the rest: **I'm THE big fat panda.**

I laugh again, and Michael's message comes in: He's sending out a search party if I'm not home in five minutes.

Gotta eat, I type. **Catch you later?**

You better :-)

Michael looks up as I burst into the kitchen. "Where've you been? You had me worried." He's ladling stew and mashed potatoes into the biggest bowl we own. He nods at my dress. "That looks new."

He sits down to eat without getting any for me.

"Not so worried that you'd serve me, too, I guess." I pile up a bowl. It smells amazing. I'd forgotten how good this feels: being properly hungry after swimming.

"Your hands aren't broken, are they?" Michael murmurs through a full mouth. But he gets up anyway and pours us both orange juice. He sets the glasses down with a thump. "Mum gave me an earful for letting you go off to Lowell on your own."

I swallow a mouthful and stare. "She called you

from *work*?" That is a first. I remember now that texts from Mum popped up while I was on You-chat. I swiped them away without reading.

"Dad spoke to her, I think. Dunno. Anyway. You're not to do it again."

"I was grand! And Jeeves was with me."

Michael doesn't return my smile. "I was worried, Ro. You were upset before, about that girl. After you left, I thought . . . I don't know what I thought." He looks at me with big eyes, like he's ready for a Dr. Phil moment.

I'm done trying to talk to him about Zara. "Don't worry yourself." I drop my bowl into the sink and head to my room. "I can handle it."

I so want to know more about Haley. With memes like hers, I bet she has mean-girl combat experience.

You there? I type, and wipe my forehead. It's still roasting in here, even with the air conditioner wheezing away.

The bubbles pop up immediately. **I'm here! I love the name Roisin, btw. Sounds like someone sweet, but also awesome.**

I laugh out loud. **Haley's cool,** I type. **Like the comet.**

There's a pause. **Halley's comet. Different spelling.**

See, I knew that, about the two *l*'s. Didn't want to come across as a brainbox. **Right, sorry,** I type. Immediately, I wince, thinking of Haley's timeline. She wouldn't apologize. She wouldn't let someone like Zara get inside her head. I scroll fast through her old posts: **If you mess with my friends, you mess with me. You don't want that.** I need to be more Haley. Or at least have someone like her in my life.

You seem kinda comet, tho, I type. **The way you come at things. Like nothing can stop you.**

:-) tysm. You're the one with the awesome name.

I'm so not awesome. The stupid tears are right there, again. I start to type that I've got to go, when Haley types back.

What makes you say that?

A million things. Crying at nothing. Letting Zara get to me. Having no friends. **There's a mean girl in my school,** I type. **I hate her.**

MEAN PEOPLE SUCK.

I know. I swallow and swipe at my eyes.

What did she do?

I've never typed so fast in my life. It's easy to tell

Haley everything. I don't know what she looks like—her manga avatar doesn't tell me much—but I picture a biggish girl like me, maybe piercings. Someone you don't mess with. Haley doesn't say it's nothing, like Michael did. She can't believe he told me to laugh it off.

Michael doesn't get it, I type. **How ANGRY Zara makes me, u know?**

I totally know.

He says I shouldn't have threatened to rip Zara's head off. But I saw that horrible poll, and I lost it.

I know how that feels, Haley types. You're like, RIP THAT HEAD OFF.

COMPLETELY OFF. There's no brain in there anyway.

You'd be doing the world a favor, she replies.

I laugh. I squish up my pillows to get comfy, and Haley and I chat and chat—I learn that she lives in Maine, and she's had mean-girl problems, too.

I haven't felt this good in ages. I'm vaguely aware of my room going orange with the setting sun, but it's only when it's so dark that my phone glows like a lamp that I realize it's probably been hours. Haley says to keep my head high tomorrow if Zara, or anyone else, pokes fun at me because of that disgusting gravy-legs meme.

If Zara says anything to your face, Haley types, look her in the eye and tell her to back off.

I hesitate. **Maybe,** I type.

You've gotta show them ur not scared, Haley types. Coral, the girl who used to harass me, now tries to be my best friend.

I roll over and stare up at my dark ceiling. I can't imagine myself talking to Zara like that. Especially if Lily's there. I've told Haley all about Lily: how our mums pushed us together, how we chatted loads, how it all fell apart. How Lily left me standing by the 7-Eleven for an hour and never showed the first weekend I arrived. How she invited me to her house, then canceled on me five minutes later.

Zara has a bestie already. Lily, remember? The one who dropped me when she saw how unpopular I am.

Ugh, that sucks. Like a hot potato? Haley includes a winky face.

I grin. Haley knows that potatoes are my soul food. **Like a radioactive potato,** I say.

Her loss, Haley says. Imagine having Zara as your bestie! Like being friends with a toxic dump.

Lol. Brb. I drop my phone. My eyes are burning,

maybe from the pool. I suddenly feel like I could sleep for a year. I flick off the air conditioner—it's still groaning but putting out no cool at all now—and flop back into bed. Without the AC's knocking hum, the quiet wraps around me.

I'm gonna crash now.

Remember what I said, right? Haley types back. **You'll be fine tomorrow.**

My stomach twists. **I don't know.**

Ro, listen. You're strong, you're gorgeous, you can do anything. Repeat after me.

I smile as I type the words back to her. She sends me a string of hearts and stars and thumbs-up.

I drop my phone and snuggle down. "Jeeves, turn off Roisin's light," I call.

The lights blink out. *"Sure!"* Jeeves speaks straight into my ear, from near my pillow, and I jump. I forgot he's on my phone now; I'm used to him on the windowsill. Jeeves the problem solver. No one can solve Zara. She's like a flesh-eating virus, dissolving me from the inside out.

"Jeeves, how do you handle bullies?"

"According to Wikipedia, ignoring it often does nothing

to stop the bullying, and it can become worse over time. Bullying behavior can be easier to control the earlier it's detected."

At least he and Haley agree. Act fast, be firm. I wish I'd known this a month ago. Or what I really wish is that they could get on the bus tomorrow instead of me.

I turn over to stare through my dark windows. One good thing about our weird flat is this room: shaped like a castle turret, with a cone roof and round walls, like something from Hogwarts. Eight-year-old me would've loved it. I do love the roundness, and the three windows that look over the roofs of Eastborough. Yellow streetlights bleed into the night, hiding the stars, but some planet sits high in the sky, clear and bright.

My heart gives a leap, remembering Haley told me to text her throughout the day tomorrow. That's what I picture as I drift off: a new friend, hundreds of miles away in the darkness but thinking of me. My own North Star.

< CHAPTER 5 >

My room's too bright, the traffic noise outside too loud. Even before my eyes open, I know I've overslept.

I kick through my covers, but my phone's nowhere. "Michael! What time is it?" No answer. He must've left already. My hands tremble as I pull on the other Urban Look dress. I'm hopping, tripping down the hall while yanking on a sandal.

A ringing finally lets me track my phone to the kitchen. It's seven forty-five: ten minutes before the bus.

Mum's face blinks up at me from the screen. She always does this: starts a video call even if you don't want to. "Morning, sweetheart." She looks as calm as I am frazzled. Her hair is tied back, the gray streak she won't dye pulling out of the ponytail at the front. Meanwhile, I look like I've been dragged through a hedge. In the video window that shows my face, my hair is a furious mass of curls, eyes gritty with sleep. Not how I want to face Zara.

I leave the phone on the table, letting Mum stare at the ceiling while I grab a granola bar and a banana. "Why didn't you wake me up?" I call toward the phone.

The churning in my belly makes me feel like I'll never eat again, but I cram the food into my backpack. It's stuffed with homework I should've done.

"I tried, twice. You just grunted." It sounds like *grunnid*. Mum's American accent is a hundred times stronger since we got here. She's on the train, of course. Why does she even come home? Forget asking for a Saturday off; she should ask for a sleeping bag and a tent so she can live at the lab. "Fixed your phone, though. The screen was locked up when I dropped in laundry last night. You loaded Jeeves onto it, finally— that's great!"

"Mum, I have to go." Eight minutes till the bus. My fingers itch to message Haley. But embarrassment suddenly surges in my chest. I kept her chatting for hours yesterday. She must think I'm a random, friend-less loser who's thrown myself at her.

"I took FRED, too, if you're looking for him. Ro, please don't leave him on your floor. I almost stepped on him."

"*It*, Mum." She's right, though. The thought of standing on that cat is *ugh*. I still think it has an evil switch I'll flick by mistake. "Okay, bye!"

"Wait—Roisin." I'm running down our hill, but Mum won't ring off. "Why don't we do something together this weekend? Michael, too. I've been so busy."

I can't think past today. "Maybe, Mum. Sure." There's something reachy in her voice that I don't rec-ognize. Like I have her attention. And she wants mine.

"That's a nice dress. Where'd it come from?"

"Um, Lowell. Urban Look." There's one instant where I nearly tell her everything: about Zara and how worthless she makes me feel, and then Lowell and swimming and meeting Jors and earning money. But it's like a gap's opened up. Mum's onshore, and I'm drifting away. In another second, the space between us will be too big to jump.

The school bus lurches up to the stop. I'm going to

try Haley. A quick, I'm-not-needy message. I flick over to You-chat—**Haley, u there?**—then back to Mum.

She's frowning. "About Lowell. Roisin, you can't run off on trains by yourself." Mum pauses. "Was it because you were desperate to go shopping? How did you have money for the dress, anyway?"

I suddenly realize that telling Mum about Jors, and that I let him do stuff to my phone, would be a super-bad idea. I mumble something about Jeeves helping me find a great bargain because he's so smart, and Mum starts explaining how she's just upgraded his problem-solving algorithm, and there are no more questions about me and money. Which is lucky, because my wallet's still missing, and Mum will go spare when she finds out. My life is basically chaos.

Hey. Haley's message pops up on top of the call with Mum. **It's Awesome Roisin.**

I laugh. My stomach still feels like a nest of snakes, but I'm so relieved to see she's online. I type fast as I climb onto the bus. **Hey! I am so glad ur around xxx**

Always here for you. Ur gonna be great today!

tysm. Just hearing that makes me feel like I can breathe. I plop down in the first empty seat.

"Roisin—are you still there?" Mum's voice blares through the bus, because I forgot to put my earbuds in. Boys in the first few seats look up. They see it's me and nudge one another. Two girls I don't know lean together to whisper, eyes pinned on me. I fumble back to the video-call screen. "Gottagobye." I stab at the red hang-up button, my heart slamming.

Too late. A ripple passes through the rows, every face looking up. The stares are suspicious, curious, hostile. My thumb automatically flicks open the main timeline of You-chat, though I don't want to look.

My stomach tumbles to the floor. Dozens more messages about me.

I was so lost in the chat with Haley last night, I forgot to check. And I did what Haley suggested: turned off notifications so I wouldn't be pinged for every horrible comment.

Hales, I type. **Have you seen what they're saying?** Tears press into my throat, threatening to burst. I scroll and scroll, trying not to care:

Did you hear crazy Irish girl got banned from TokTalk? . . . I heard she tried to fight Zara in WholeFoods. Mara tried to stop her so Rosheen HIT her. And Zara's

reply: **She's trash. She definitely hurt Mara. Told u. She's crazy.**

I sink lower in the front seat, hugging my phone.

Aw, hun, Haley replies. **Ignore them.**

I swallow hard. **I wish u didn't live in Maine,** I say. I'd give anything to have Haley by my side, to help me face down these lies.

I know, it sucks.

She has no idea. I scroll through more comments. A stone feels like it's lodged in my throat. Zara's the one who attacks me, every day. But now she's turned it around and made me the bad guy. I keep my face forward as the bus rumbles on, but the whispers have started behind me: "Ro-SHEEN. Ro-SHEEN. Ro-SHEEN." Like dry trees ready to catch fire.

Here's how Haley handled her mean girls in Old Orchard Beach. That's where her school is in Maine, three hours from here—which might as well be on the moon when you're car-less like us. Haley says the worst was Coral, a skinny girl who sat at her table in Home Economics. She slagged off Haley the whole time. Never right to her face, but what Coral said was always meant for Haley, like, *"Don't you hate it when people DON'T WASH THEIR FACE?"* Which is crazy unfair, because Haley uses that Fresh 'n' Clean face wash four times a day, she told me. It's just that her skin is oily—not her fault! And who doesn't have skin things to worry about?

But Haley worried about it loads, until it got to a point where she felt sick in the morning, started skipping school, was shaking in the halls when she did go. Then it got worse. Coral started tripping Haley up, pinching her . . . until the day Coral brought in her baby brother's dirty diaper and left it in Haley's locker. When Haley found it, Coral was right there and whispered in her ear, *"Ew, EVERYTHING about you is dirty, isn't it?"*

That's horrendous, I type. **What did you do?** I'm in the girls' loos, sending Haley my zillionth help-me message today, and it's only third period. It's a relief to have something else to focus on. Poor Haley. I can't believe that Coral girl was such a witch. **I hope you kicked her into next week.**

There's a pause. **I grabbed her hair and smashed her into the lockers.**

Whoa. Serious? I blink at my phone. I was joking. **Do you give lessons? JK**, I add quickly. I'm still getting the nerve to look Zara in the eye, never mind smash her.

Is that what you want to do? Haley answers.

I can't find the words. Haley and Jeeves and everyone says I have to act fast to stop Zara. But no way can I lay a hand on her. It'd just make everyone believe the lies about me, that I'm the bully. Before I can think of what to say, the bell shrieks for fourth period and I jump a mile. **Gtg**, I type.

I push out of the stall to wash my hands and stop short. Lily is fixing her eyeliner. Her face lights when she sees me. "There you are!"

I look at my hands, saying nothing as I soap into gray lather. We've had three classes together already. Lily keeps trying to talk to me, but I've slipped away. I can't face her fake friendliness, or whatever it is. And Zara is her personal bodyguard, vibing me to back off.

"Are you okay?" Lily's forehead is creased into that I-really-care frown. Spare me. "Listen, there's something I need to—"

Just then, the girls' room door bursts open. Zara and Mara blow in like bad weather, a swirl of giggles and grapefruit body mist. We've all just had Gym together, where Zara gave me the evil eye so hard in the changing room, she practically burned a hole through my skull. Nothing better than stripping down to your underpants in front of someone who hates you.

"Lily, guess WHAT?" Mara starts jabbering about Nikesh, and the field trip next week, and how he wants to sit with Lily on the bus.

I try to get past Zara, who's blocking the way out. My liquid legs barely carry me. She's so tiny. I'm pathetic. But I remember what Haley said, about looking Zara in the eye. I lift my head.

"Move," I say. It comes out as a whisper.

"Or what?" Zara says. But she chews her lip and stands aside. "It's not an improvement, freak," she murmurs as I go. "That dress."

I am a bad person, I type to Haley. **A violent person.** Thank God Almighty, today has passed. Somehow. My wallet's still missing, my homework isn't done, and everyone in Eastborough thinks I tried to fight Zara and Mara. But I'm finally back in the only place I feel safe: my room, with Haley. Someone should carve her a monument. Every time I say how nothing Zara makes me feel, Haley lifts me up. Tells me I'm smarter, stronger. Kinder.

Why do you say that? U haven't touched Zara! Ur too hard on yourself, Ro.

But all I can think about is Zara being wiped off the face of the earth.

Is that what you want?

No! I just want to stop feeling like this.

Well, you know how to make a start with that: like we said.

This is what we've spent most of the afternoon plotting: assertive things I can say to Zara so that I don't spend tomorrow hiding from her, like today. Even looking her in the eye was a big deal. Haley says I just need to tell her to back off. But part of me wants to humiliate her like she's done to me. Zara doesn't have the best grades. It'd be so easy to cut her down, make her feel small. But that's not me. Is it?

"Roisin?" calls a distant voice. "Roisin!"

I jump off the bed.

My heart thumps like a drum. There's only one person who says my name right. I rush to my window.

Lily is standing in our front garden, frowning up. Her face clears when she spots me, and she waves.

The window is jammed, but it finally opens with a scream of old wood. "What are you doing here?" It's out of my mouth before I hear how hostile it sounds.

But Lily just smiles and holds up my wallet. "I didn't know which was your doorbell, so . . ." She shrugs.

"I'm coming down." I can't believe Lily, of all people, found my wallet. I tell Haley not to go, that Lily's here and I'll brb, and I tear downstairs.

"Hey!" Lily stands at the front door, with that open smile everyone loves. Her hair hangs over one shoulder, a roll of black satin. The sunset angles in from the side, arranging itself to make Lily look like a painting. I'm extra-aware of my insane hair: The humidity has puffed the curls, like an Irish Einstein. "Thought you might need this. You're not easy to get ahold of."

Oh no. My cheeks burn. "Is that why you were trying to catch up with me today?" I squeeze out our screen door and it slaps closed behind me.

She nods. "Messaged you, too. Guess you didn't see it?"

I haven't gone near my DMs apart from Haley.

"Sorry," I murmur. "Thanks a million." Part of me worries that this is a setup, that Zara's hiding in a bush, laughing. But one look at Lily shows she's genuine. Maybe lost things just flow toward her, like she has her own gravity. "Did you find it on the road?" The wallet's dirty but otherwise looks fine: the same green lump I thought I'd tucked safely into my swim bag yesterday.

"Nikesh did." Lily stands with her arms around her middle. I should invite her in. But the thought of her seeing our home, its shabby furniture . . . I can't.

"Well, tell him thanks. I dropped it running for the train."

Lily nods. "I love trains."

"Same. 'I LIKE TRAINS,'" I say absentmindedly. It's a meme from years ago. Lily laughs, and I smile. There it is: This is how it felt on You-chat, when we first met. Trading dumb jokes and stories about our annoying mums.

The moment passes. We go quiet, but Lily lingers on our porch. I can feel that she wants to connect, like Michael when he tries to cheer me up.

My phone buzzes, and we both look at it: Haley,

asking where I am. I'm dying to get back to her, too. I can't explain it. It's not just that she's funny and smart. It's how she makes me feel about *me*—like I might be funny and smart, too. Lily's the opposite. Next to someone so bright, you can't help feeling dim.

Lily watches me shove my phone into my dress pocket, and wrinkles crease her forehead. She points to two ancient Adirondack chairs on the veranda. "Can we talk for a sec?"

"All right." She sits. I perch on the edge of the other weird chair. I've imagined this for ages: Lily hanging at my house. But it's like sitting on nails. Zara would lose it if she saw us right now.

"I'm sorry about Zara and Mara." Lily looks at her clasped hands. "I have no idea what their problem is."

I do.

"That was super mean, what they did with the Goodwill bag—and all the stuff online." She stares at me. "I'm guessing you didn't attack either of them, like people are saying?"

I shake my head. "I bumped into Mara by mistake, that's all." Lily looks miserable, and I feel the strangest pain—guilt, I think. I've dragged storm clouds into her storybook life. It's not a story I belong in. I'm too weird, too unpopular. If she wanted to be friends, why did she keep standing me up when I first got here? Leaving me waiting around, telling me I got the wrong time when she's the one who made the plans? "Forget about it." I stand up.

Lily doesn't. "They're coming over tomorrow after school. You should, too. If you guys got to know each other . . ."

I swallow. "I don't think so."

"Come on, my dad got the pool cleaned. It'll be fun."

It will not. I picture Zara and Mara stretched by the pool, skimpy bikinis and faces full of makeup. My phone buzzes again in my pocket. Lily winces. I realize she thinks it's more notifications from Zara's horrible posts. She doesn't know it's Haley.

"It's tough when you have no—" Lily breaks off. "When you don't know anyone."

My cheeks go hot; she was about to say, *"When you have no friends."* I want to tell her about Sophie and Maisie back in Ireland, my friends from the swim club, all the people who liked me. And about Haley: someone who thinks I'm brilliant. Someone who has no time for mean girls. Unlike Lily, who surrounds herself with them.

Lily stands. "Promise me you'll think about it." A royal command. We don't think much of those where I come from.

I say nothing. Silence weighs down the air between us. I open our screen door. "Thanks again for bringing my wallet."

"Sure." Lily turns and goes. "See you tomorrow." She sounds so cheery, like I'm not the rudest person she's ever met.

"Bye," I mumble when Lily's too far away to hear. Her long shadow goes ahead of her down our hill.

I start typing to Haley again as I climb our stairs.

Yay, hi! she says. I thought you forgot about me :-(

Not a chance. I smile. It's a nice feeling, being wanted. I told you I dropped my wallet? Lily brought it back.

Queen Lily? Is this the girl who was like, "oh, come over to my house! No, wait, don't"?

That's the one. Her boyfriend found it on the road. She invited me to her pool party. Zara and Mara are going.

Ha! That'd be super fun, right?

I bet Zara doesn't even know Lily invited me, I type. **She'd have a jealous fit.**

You said no, I hope?

Yeah, I told her no. But even as I type it, a niggle scratches at me. I can't figure out why Lily is making such an effort. **Lily's nice, tho. Unless she's really, really good at faking it.**

Yeah. She could be laughing at you, under a fake layer of nice. Forget Lily. U ready to handle Zara?

We go over everything again before saying good night. It's early, but I can't keep my eyes open. The dying sun turns my walls red as it lowers itself onto the roofs of Eastborough. I wonder which one Zara sleeps under. Or whether she sleeps; maybe she's always awake, brainstorming how to skewer me.

My heart thumps hard suddenly, and I grab my phone again. Haley's given me some power phrases to say to Zara. I'm sure I'm remembering them wrong. There's a few, from the back-off type all the way to shredding-her smackdowns. But when I flick over to You-chat, the app's frozen, and even rebooting my phone doesn't fix it. I toss it to the end of my bed and stare at the curved ceiling. My stomach gives a long, nervy squawk.

Maybe, if I do what Haley says, Zara will respect me, like I've passed some sick test. But I might just make it all worse. The red drains from my room, taking my courage with it. I curl up tight in the sheets, but Zara's face paints itself across my eyelids.

My brain keeps trying to imagine how Zara will react if I confront her. So I barely notice when sleep comes, with the dreams of Zara, now a foot taller than me, slamming me against my locker.

Everyone watches, filming it on their phones, saying nothing.

‹ CHAPTER 6 ›

It's last period of the worst day of my life. I've hardly looked at Zara, never mind been assertive. For the second day straight, stares and whispers of *diarrhea* and *psycho* have followed me everywhere. At lunch, instead of the usual loser circle of empty seats around me, there was a whole empty table. Lily tried—I think—to give me sympathy looks across the cafeteria, but it didn't help. And it was runny beef stew for lunch. Zara laughed through it all, tossing me I-own-you looks or whispering as she went by: "Gross."

I just want her to SHUT UP, I type. I'm hiding in the loos again. I should be in Art, but we're still drawing our partners' portraits. The world wants me to suffer. Clueless Mr. Morrison keeps making encouraging sounds about my sketch of Zara when he passes. He doesn't hear what she's hissed at me all period: *"Is there a smell in here? I can smell something."*

You know this is all because Zara is SUPER JEALOUS, right? Haley says. **Cuz Lily's invited you to her party etc. Zara sounds totally insecure.**

Haley, who is the best person, has to keep telling her teacher she has a stomachache, so she can nip out of class to chat to me; she says she doesn't mind.

I should let you go, I type. **I'm going to get you in trouble.** I don't know what I'll do if Haley's teacher takes her phone. I clutch my forehead and haul in a breath. The stink of the toilet stall is foul, but it fits my mood.

It's fine, Haley says. **If you need to talk, I'm here whenever. You matter more than Chemistry.**

Her words make the tears climb my throat again. How can one girl be so awesome and another be such a virus?

I hate her I hate her I hate her, I type. **She deserves to get smashed, like you did Coral.**

You could do that. She'd know you're not messing around. Sometimes the only thing they understand is force.

I let myself picture it: my hand with a fistful of Zara's hair. But I kick the image away. I'm not going to become what they're already saying I am. **That's not me, Hales.**

Says the girl who wanted to rip heads off. Anyway, you don't have to hurt her. Just make her think you will.

Gtg, I type. **xxx cya later?** I can't talk about this anymore. The tears are right there, and I won't go back to Art with swollen eyes. I slip my phone back into my dress pocket, but it's not till I'm at the sinks that I realize one of the other stalls is occupied.

Zara's shoes.

My heart pounds so hard, it thuds in my throat. Her stall whooshes open and I flinch, I can't help it. I keep my back to her, praying she'll say nothing. My eyes dart to the mirrors.

"Hey!" Zara smiles. It's so much worse than her usual puckered glare. "Mr. Morrison sent me to find you. You've been in here *forever.*" She shows me her fancy smartwatch, like I care. The honey in her voice is like a spider up my back. I flick off the tap and snatch at the paper towels. My hands tremble. I feel the warmth of my phone in my dress pocket. I tell myself it's Haley, urging me to be strong. I don't want to be strong, I want to get out of here, but Zara stands between me and the door.

"Lily says she invited you to her pool party." She leans against the sinks and tilts her head. "You know it's just because her mom made her, right? Because your mom works with her?" I'm drying my hands, rubbing them red, but this stops me. That hadn't even occurred to me. My stomach falls away. I bet Zara's right. It was our mums who pushed us together on You-chat in the first place. "If you go, you'll just embarrass yourself." She snaps her fingers in front of my face. "Maybe look at people when they talk to you? So they don't think you're *rude*."

Raising my head feels like the hardest thing I've ever done, but I drag my eyes up to Zara's.

The bathroom door sweeps open. In walks Mara, with another girl from the fringes of their lunch-table group: dark eyes, black ponytail. They're silent, and Zara doesn't even look around. Like she was expecting them. They circle behind me.

The hairs on my neck prickle. Fear makes words burst out of me.

"I don't give a toss what you think." My voice is tight, high. "And I'll do what I like. Let me out."

Zara's eyebrows lift, but she stays put, arms crossed. A smile pulls up one side of her mouth. "You know you can't go to a pool party unless you're clean. Isn't that right, Mar?" Her eyes go to Mara behind me.

Mara snorts. "I don't think she's clean."

Zara sighs, like it's a shame. "I don't think she *wipes*."

I launch myself toward the door and freedom. Zara yelps and fear flicks over her face, like I'm making a lunge for her.

I'm hauled backward suddenly, hot hands hooked through my elbows.

"Get away from her, you freak show!" Mara's voice is in my ear. The girl gripping my other elbow, still silent, has superhuman strength. They pull my arms back so far, the buttons on my new dress threaten to pop. The thought of them laughing at me, my dress ripped open . . . I swallow. I'm wearing my worst bra, white-turned-gray, with the ripped lace. A flush creeps up my neck, burning my cheeks.

Zara scrapes a rattail of hair away from her face with a nail. She doesn't look scared now. Her eyes glint like bullets. "We need to check if you're clean enough for the pool."

Mara hoots her laugh.

My stomach turns to ice.

No—they can't do this. I'm hyper-aware of my bare legs, and where the cotton hem ends above my knees.

"I bet she doesn't even change her underwear," Zara says thoughtfully, and paces toward me.

I thrash, but they hold me tight. My sandals slide on the slippy tiles. There are three of them. If they try to pull up my dress, I can't stop them.

Silent girl lets me go. My right arm is free! I shove Mara off me.

"What's your problem, Nita?" Zara scowls. Silent Nita shakes her head so hard, her black ponytail swings. She pushes through the bathroom door without a word.

I'm right behind her, but Nita's already disappeared down the corridor. My breathing slows, and I lean against a wall. My cheeks still blaze, but I'm shivering. The bell screams its ring and classroom doors burst open, pouring people. The Friday crush to escape is desperate. I force my legs to move, pushing against the flow to get back into Art for my bag, and stumble through the classroom door.

"You all right?"

I flinch at the hand on my shoulder. Mr. Morrison looks worried; the frown creases his whole stubbly head.

I nod. But my hand trembles as I pick up my bag. He passes me a sketchpad, and I stare at it before I realize it's my own drawing.

"Great work today. Why don't you take it home this weekend, show your folks?"

In the picture, Zara's mouth is twisted in that half-smile.

I turn away. There's wet in my mouth, like I'm ready to be sick on the floor. Mr. Morrison is still asking if I'm all right when I walk out the door.

The bus ride home is a numb nothing. The feel of Mara and Nita holding my arms flashes back every few seconds. I crouch on the plasticky seat, hoping to die. With every bump of the bus, I imagine that's me lying under it, *thump thump*. Crushed. Problems over.

Until my phone buzzes in my bag: Haley, asking how it went, did I talk to Zara.

Ugly tears pour down my face. I'm past caring who sees me. **Awful. The worst. She's A PIG.**

Aw, sweetie, Haley says. **I would hug you right now if I could. Tell me everything.**

I start telling her what happened. I don't even remember getting off the bus. All I know is that sympathy shines out of Haley like a light, and I follow it. Thank God for her.

Two hours later, I feel a billion times better—apart from my thumbs, which ache from messaging. We've gone over every detail of my nightmare day: from the *psycho* whispers to the attack in the bathroom.

But what we talk about most is how Zara should be punished.

She should be covered in scabby pus sores, Haley says. **Like the plague rat she is.**

I nod as I type. **A rock should fall from space and flatten her in her bed.**

SHE should fall from space, Haley says.

Into boiling oil.

Or sharks. Sharks are always good.

I laugh and stretch on my bed. I rack my brains for a new idea, but we've covered most of the ways Zara should suffer. Then I remember the glint of her smart-watch under the bathroom lights. **Can you get shocked by a smartwatch?** I say. I picture Zara's perfect straight hair frizzing up, worse than mine. **Maybe if she wore it in the bath.**

Zara has a smartwatch? What kind?

I'm typing when there's a quick knock on my bed-room door, and it swishes open. I sit up and scowl. "It's called privacy, Michael."

"Ready to go?"

It's Mum. I'm so floored, I just stare. "What are you doing home?" My phone says five fifteen p.m. Mum hasn't come home in daylight since we got here. My mind races to all kinds of tragedies and I stand. "Is Dad okay?"

"Wow, it's hot in here." Mum sweeps over to the window. "Why isn't the AC on?" She's her neat self: auburn hair pulled back, trim skirt, and tucked-in blouse. She's changed out of her commute shoes and is in heels, for some reason. "Everything's fine with Dad. Why aren't you ready?"

She tugs at the window, which is still stuck open from yesterday, when Lily visited. With an expert thump and a slap, Mum gets the window down and flicks on the AC. Her eyes sweep my room. She's making a giant effort not to comment on the dirty clothes by the bin, and the clean laundry I haven't put away. "Is that what you're wearing?"

"What are you talking about?"

Mum sighs. "Don't even tell me you haven't seen my messages."

I look at the phone in my hand. A few texts have popped up, but I've been busy.

Mum's eyes roll to the ceiling. "Jeeves, read Roisin's messages."

My phone buzzes as Jeeves pipes up. *"Sure! Four messages received from Kathryn Doyle. Three forty-five p.m. today: 'Hey, Roisin, we're heading to a cookout later; can you be ready by five?' Four fifteen p.m. today: 'Roisin, did you get my message? Let me—'"*

I get the point. "Jeeves, stop." I huff and try to do something to my hair. The waves bounce and pull against the brush. I text Haley that I've gtg, and Mum whooshes out my door.

It's not until we're outside in the cab, where I'm sandwiched between a giant striped bag that Mum has plonked there and Michael—who's man-spreading like crazy—that Mum twists around from the front seat and beams at us.

"This'll be fun!"

"*What*, Mum?" I look at Michael, but he gives me a frozen grin, like a robot who's been instructed to express happiness.

"Remember, I said yesterday: We should do something as a family this weekend. We're going to a family cookout."

"Whose family?" Mum's not listening; she's talking to the driver. We've hardly gone any distance before the cab stops outside the nicest house in Eastborough: all wooden shutters and flowering trees. Lexus in the driveway. Historic plaque by the door, where Lily is standing with her father.

I can't believe this.

"My boss's," Mum murmurs, opening the cab door. "Be nice."

"Welcome! Some weather today, huh?" Lily's dad has the best smile: I can see where she gets it from. Seeing him throws me, though, because he looks Japanese. I knew Lily was mixed race, but I was pretty sure it was her mum who was from Japan.

Lily's dad puts out his hand. "Kathryn. Great to meet you, finally! I'm Brian Tanaka; this is my daughter, Lily. Everyone's out back." There's a lot of shuffling. Mum introduces me and Michael while she fishes in the striped bag for the wine we brought. We crowd through the front door. Lily's big brother is there, too. More introductions.

It's unreal to be standing in Lily's house at last. Everything is classy New England: polished wooden steps lead upstairs, and a lamp on the hall table spreads a stained-glass glow up the wall. We pass a family room that makes ours look like a sad hotel. I glimpse leather couches and a gigantic flat screen. Michael turns to give me a did-you-see-that-monster-TV stare, but my mind is too blown.

Not only has Mum dragged us to her boss's house, pretending it's family time, but now I have to make stupid small talk with Lily, who I have nothing to say to anymore. Zara is basically Satan. If Lily can't see that, she's no better. My jaw clenches as we follow Lily. Her glossy hair shines in the glare bouncing into the house from the back garden.

I stop short. Splashing and shrieky laughter leak in from outside. Oh God oh God. This is Lily's pool party. Starring Zara and Mara. My heartbeat hammers in my throat. Sweat pricks under my arms and I tug at the hem of my dress, pulling it lower over my bare legs.

"Mum!" I lean past Michael and clutch her arm. "We don't have swimsuits; I'll go back for them." I'll walk up our hill dead slow, poke around at home getting our things; maybe the devil twins will be gone by the time I get back.

"Got everything right here." Mum pats the black-and-white bag on her shoulder. I stare helplessly at its prison stripes. Of course Mum is organized, and there is no escape.

‹ CHAPTER 7 ›

It's impossible to ignore them, but I've tried. They're stretched on sun loungers like roasting meat, Zara rubbing oil onto her arms. Her suit is a one-piece, Day-Glo green against her perfect tan. Even Mara, in her stringy bikini, is a pleasing apricot gold: I'd thought her blonde hair meant she'd be pale like me. I'm standing under the parasol, smearing on sunscreen that turns my ghost legs bluish-white, when I hear them snicker.

Here we go. This'll be about me, whatever they're laughing at. An image of the virus we saw in Biology jumps into my brain. I can see my entire future in Eastborough: Zara infecting everything, spreading, getting stronger.

"Is that your *brother*?" Zara's voice bubbles with a held-back laugh.

I look at Michael, standing by the door of the pool house, where he's just changed. He's fiddling with the tie to his swimsuit.

Lily's brother, Hiro, hoists himself out of the pool. He pads past Zara and Mara, baggy trunks streaming water, and flicks a hand to make them shriek. Zara roots in her bag for her phone, wide eyes fixed on Michael. What is the big deal?

Zara smirks and starts to say something to me, but I jam in my earplugs. Her voice becomes a thick mumble.

Flashbacks of the bathroom stab through me: slippy floor tiles, hands gripping my arms. But I listen to my breathing, the loudness of it. And I reach for what Haley said: the next time you see those girls, do this, right? Picture a plate of armor across ur chest. You are so much better than them.

I dive in with barely a splash, and cool silence swallows me. The underwater is mine, and the dappled light. I glide, streamlined, to the far end, then tumble-turn without a breath.

I don't know how many laps I do, but I'm in my zone and almost forget the trolls at poolside. I do my strokes, imagining more tragedies striking Zara, from getting a face full of pimples to falling out the door of an airplane. I need to remember them, to tell Haley. Each one makes me feel stronger, like driving a nail through what happened in the bathroom.

Two sets of baggy trunks cannonball into the deep end, their tucked bodies trailing bubbles.

I surface, panting. It's a second before Michael and Hiro come up. "Why'd you change?" I ask him. Michael's trying to stand on Hiro's shoulders, and he's wearing weird trunks: not his Speedos, but loose folds of yellow and blue.

Michael stands up slowly and stretches his arms out for balance. "Borrowed these from Hiro. The others were ripped."

"And a little *wrong*," Hiro says, grinning. His shoulders shake with Michael's weight, but he looks older than Michael, and even broader. Streaming water flattens Hiro's hair around his eyes, and he looks so like one of Haley's manga heartthrobs, I want to take a picture for her.

"Wrong!" Michael echoes, and they both laugh like hyenas. This is my brother; he only just met Hiro, and they're friends. Michael topples off with a gigantic splash, and that's when I notice the empty sun loungers: Zara and Mara have vanished, and their stuff is gone. Relief avalanches over me.

There's another splash. "Hey!" Lily bursts out of the water, pushing her hair back. "Omigod! That feels so good; I was burning up. Sorry I abandoned you. Mom made me pass out drinks while she grills. She won't let anyone else touch her *tare* marinade." Lily nods toward the barbecue, surrounded by people from Mum's work: rumpled geeks who don't leave the lab much, or ever. A dozen or so of them stand around with beers, not drinking, talking hard.

My eyes go back to the poolside. "Where's, um . . ." Zara's name sticks in my throat. I pray she's gone, but maybe she's lying in wait somewhere.

"Zara had to babysit her brother, so they headed out."

I tread water and Lily ducks under to do a handstand. Suddenly I hear birds singing, or maybe they were there all along. I couldn't be happier if Lily had said, *"Here, have this bag of money."*

Savory smells waft from the smoking grill. That's when I do a double take, because the crowd's moved and I get my first look at Lily's mother. She must be the one in the apron, deep in conversation with my mother, gesturing with long tongs. She's smiley, shorter than Mum, and white. She's even paler than I am.

This is so odd, I forget all about being cool to Lily like I'd planned. "Your mum . . . is from Tokyo? I didn't think—" I stop and shake my head. "Ugh, do I sound like some mad racist? I didn't know there were white Japanese people."

Lily shrugs. "Mom was born in Japan, grew up speaking English and Japanese. She went to an international school in Tokyo, but she says she's Japanese on the inside." Lily flips over and swims on her back toward the edge. I wonder how often she's had this chat, about her mum's background. I feel like an idiot for mentioning it. But Lily's her sunny self. She climbs out and sits beside the drinks tray; it's empty except for one can and her smartwatch. "Saved you a lemonade, if you want it?"

"Thanks." I heave out of the pool, and the sun warms my back. I sip my drink and give a sigh so huge,

Lily bursts out laughing. I can't help it: I smile, too. The whole world is lighter with those two sun loungers empty. We dangle our legs, and I hold up my lemonade. "I'd have thought you'd have a robot to pass out drinks."

Her eyes stretch huge. "We actually do!"

"Ha! Serious?" I try to picture a robot butler rolling over the lawn, around the lilac bushes.

"Yes! He's broken. Hiro tried to make him carry his dumbbells. Hey!" Lily starts, like she's remembered something. "You are amazing in the pool. Did you swim on a team?"

I feel a blush creep up. "My school's, in Dublin."

"Hiro swims front crawl for Amherst."

I don't know what Amherst is—a university? He must be good.

"He's amazing. Just finished freshman year. Hence all this." She gestures around. "I'm psyched you came, Roisin. Even if, you know . . . your mom made you."

She says it like she's not the queen in her castle, like I'm doing her a favor. And here's the crazy Lily thing: She sounds like she means it. The sarcastic comeback I want to fling at her just vanishes. Instead I go for the truth. "I've wanted to come to yours for ages, Lily." I study my lemonade can. "That sounds needy, sorry."

"Really?" Lily gives me a long look. "Okay, just that—you canceled on me a few times, and I thought . . ."

"*I* canceled?"

She turns around to face me. "We were going to meet at the 7-Eleven, the Saturday you arrived. You were too tired, I get that, but then you didn't come over that next week when I— *Oh*." Lily's face drops. Her hand covers her mouth. "Oh, Roisin."

What she says next should make me furious, but I'm too stunned. Lily explains that Zara takes her phone sometimes. She's sent messages before, pretending to be Lily. Just for fun.

Lily stands up. "You know what? Let's check that right now. Where's your phone?"

Lily follows me to the pool house, and I dig out my phone from the clothes pile. Bingo. Roisin! You around Saturday? Come at 2 if you can. It's an old DM from Lily, and right after it, the cancellation. Sorry! My mom says no one can come over.

Lily stares miserably at me through the gloom of the pool house. "I never sent that. And it was Zara who told me you'd called and said you were too jet-lagged to meet that first weekend. She said she answered my phone because I was in the bathroom."

I shake my head. I feel like laughing. That first weekend was the time I told Haley about: when I stood for ages at the 7-Eleven, waiting for Lily. Later, she texted to say I'd got the time wrong. Only that was Zara, too: more fake messages.

"Wow," I say. "She is just— Wow." Haley is utterly right. Zara is so insecure about Lily's friendship that she's lied left, right, and center—lied to me and about me.

Two skimmer nets for cleaning the pool lean on the wall behind Lily. Their giant see-through heads on stick bodies remind me of Zara and Mara, whispering in the hall.

"I'm so, so sorry." Lily shakes her head and bites her lip.

I feel like a ton of weight has rolled off me. Lily's mum didn't make her invite me. She wants me here.

Outside I can hear Michael and Hiro still goofing around in the pool. Michael yells at me to come get my butt kicked in a game of chicken. I'm not going to let someone as flimsy as Zara ruin what could be a fab party.

I drop my phone onto my clothes. "Come on." I yank Lily back outside. "We have some brothers to beat."

We splash and shout and mess about in the pool for ages, and finally we relay race. I come this close to beating Hiro, and the others give me such a cheer, I feel like I'm at a swimming competition again. Michael makes me stand high on his shoulders, and he shouts that I've won a silver, and the others applaud, and this feeling . . . this feeling floods me that I thought was gone forever: Everything is okay.

"Hello! You must be the next generation of Doyles." Lily's mum stands with the tongs at poolside, smiling down. Her voice is like Lily's, but with a British tinge. You wouldn't know she's from Tokyo. Lily does introductions. Her mum nods that it's lovely to meet us, and are we ready to eat?

Lily makes a face, like she'd rather keep swimming, but nods. Hiro vaults out of the pool and threatens to soak his mum with a hug. She laughs and swipes at him with the tongs, calling out something in Japanese. She hands us towels and her blue eyes study me. "Hungry?"

Is it okay to say I'm starving? The aroma of roasting meat is so luscious, I could eat the air. "Definitely. And it smells *so* good."

Her mum beams, and Lily smiles at me as she straps her watch back on. I said the right thing.

The rest of the barbecue is great. We stuff ourselves from platters of teriyaki beef and sesame chicken, then play Nintendo on the giant TV and squashy couches, wrapped in cozy after-swim clothes that Mum, of course, packed. I catch her watching me from the center of a group of lab people. Their beer bottles are empty now, and they're a lot noisier. Mum's look says, *I knew you'd sulk if I told you this was a work thing, but this is good, right?* I don't give her anything, just turn back to the TV and our game; it's annoying enough, being dragged along by the tide of Mum-knows-best. She doesn't get smiley-me, too, even if this afternoon was brilliant.

Lily shows me her room. She owns every good thing: shelves to the ceiling with more books than a library, a walk-in closet, and a mirror with bulbs around it, like a celeb's dressing room. Wait till I tell Haley.

She already thinks Lily is a spoiled princess. I realize I haven't messaged Haley in hours. She'll think I died.

I spot a pinboard that makes me go cold. Old photos of Lily and Zara, instant printouts from those retro cameras everyone wanted a few years ago. Every picture is a square of perfect: blazing sun, impossible blue skies, ultra-green grass. I look at one of Zara and Lily at the beach, shouting, jumping, hair flying.

"That's fourth grade, when she still lived in Maine."

I make a sound that I hope makes it clear I don't want to talk about Zara. Even Lily seemed more relaxed after Zara and Mara left. But now it's like some loyalty thing's kicked in, because she wants to tell me where every picture was taken. I turn away from the pinboard while she's still talking. Lily trails off. "Zara's really nice," she says quietly. "She used to be, anyway."

Really nice?

"Zara had two girls hold me so I couldn't move in the bathroom." The words tumble out; I don't remember telling my mouth to speak. "She came at me. Said she was going to pull up my dress and check inside my underpants." I stare at Lily's dresser. Lacquer-red jewelry box. Scuffed nail file. Spare strap for her watch, the hole at the center like a missing eye. I realize I've stopped breathing and make myself pull in air.

"Oh," Lily says finally. "My God."

I begin to shake, freezing suddenly despite my hoodie. In the mirror, I see Lily start to reach for my shoulder, pull her hand back, cover her mouth. "You should tell somebody."

This floors me. I open my mouth to say I *am* telling—I'm telling her! But just then an alarm screams; a wail like the world is ending. *TEEE TEEE TEEE.*

Lily rolls her eyes. Her smartwatch is talking to her. She holds it against her ear. She shouts to me over the wailing alarm and points downstairs. "I think we should . . . !"

I'm guessing the house isn't actually on fire, but it's the excuse Lily wants to get away from this conversation. She rushes out of the room.

I follow her down the shrieking hall. Bitterness boils in my stomach. Does she have any idea how hard that was? Telling her what Zara did? And she doesn't want to know. If I'd told Michael, he would've hugged me till I couldn't breathe. Not Lily.

She turns at the top of the stairs, her watch pressed

to her ear. The *TEEE TEEE TEEE* stops suddenly. "Taiko says it's smoke in the kitchen, someone burning food. But it's okay now." I guess Taiko is their Jeeves? A few minutes ago, when I thought we were becoming friends, I would've asked her about it. Not now. Lily says something in Japanese to Taiko—the lights switch off behind us—and she smiles at me, like everything's fine.

Like that meme, the dog sitting in cartoon flames: "THIS IS FINE." Lily's just heard that Zara does way more than take her phone and send fake messages. She's the worst kind of bully. But it's not even a blip on the radar of Lily's shiny life.

I am super rude for our last five minutes at the party. Michael won't leave Hiro or even look up from the Nintendo until I swear so bad, Michael whistles and makes googly eyes.

Lily's mum sees us to the door. I hardly look at her, though she says nice things: She was glad Hiro and Michael got on so well, and she was especially happy to meet me. I was kind to come over after school, she says, to help Lily with geometry. I'm about to say that was Nikesh, not me, but I feel Lily tense opposite me.

The panic's obvious in her eyes: I guess her mum will flip if she finds out Lily has a boyfriend. And I'm her alibi.

"You're a math whiz, Lily tells me," her mum says. "Thanks for helping her."

"It's fine." I study my shoes. I should betray Lily, like she did me. But I don't.

Lily's mum makes a *hmm* sound and looks at Lily. Silence falls and doesn't lift while we wait for Mum. Even Michael is quiet. A tray of brightly painted wooden birds sits on the hall table. Michael fiddles with a bird. Years pass.

There's a sudden waft of laughter and burnt smell as the kitchen door swings open. I glimpse a geek in oven gloves giggling at a tray of something black and smoking. Mum calls goodbye and follows Mr. Tanaka to the front door, both of them grinning.

Mum instantly susses out the thick silence and starts babbling: about the party, the food, their lovely, lovely home. Her boss starts to look uncomfortable at all the compliments. *Mum, STOP TALKING*, I beg silently, but she revs up when she's nervous.

"Put that back, Michael. Ooh, that's exquisite—

where did you get them?" Mum takes the tiny carving from Michael and peers at it before passing it to Mr. Tanaka. His open smile wobbles. He places the bird carefully on the hall table again, not answering.

Mum shuts up, finally, and somehow we get out the door. It closes behind us. Michael helps Mum down the slick path in her heels; the bricks gleam in the drizzle that's begun to fall. Part of me believes Lily will come through—throw open the door, tell me she's sorry—but there's only silence, and darkness.

‹ CHAPTER 8 ›

You're never totally friendless, or at least you don't look it, if you have your phone. Haley and I message each other nonstop on the bus ride to the museum for my field trip Monday morning. I know I should let her go, so she can do school-whatever, but Haley says her Chem teacher is clueless; she could stand on her head and he wouldn't notice. That girl can make me laugh.

After two hours, though, I need to switch off. Nausea sloshes in my stomach.

Carsick, sorry! It's not just my tummy. The head-ache I've had all weekend is getting worse. **Ughhhhhh. Talk to u later?**

Deffo!

I grin. **You're sounding Irish yourself.**

Ha! Good! Cya later Ro.

I press my palms against my eyes. I'm stretched out, legs and bag along the front seat. It's not like anyone wanted to sit with me, anyway. I lean back into the cool of the window. I should've stopped looking at my screen sooner, but Haley's all I have. We keep saying it's a tragedy that I can't move to Old Orchard Beach. I'd do it in a heartbeat.

A shrieky laugh from behind me is like a knife through my brain. Just like that, the warm feeling of talking to Haley ices over.

I risk a glance. Three rows back, Lily sits with Nikesh. She twists around to Zara as I watch: Zara and Mara sit behind her and want to show Lily something on the phone. Lily gives the screen a quick smile and turns away, but the others roar laughing at whatever they're watching. Probably someone suffering on YouTube, those awful videos where toddlers get whacked by falling Christmas trees. Zara cries with laughter. What kind of world is it, where she gets to be this happy?

What an idiot I was, to think those two feel-good hours at Lily's house were my life. Before she left the party to go babysit, Zara had already plotted my next punishment, though I didn't know it yet.

On Saturday morning, it had all kicked off. Michael nudged into my room, waggling his phone. I'd hardly slept, and a headache pounded through my skull, but Michael was grinning. Zara had posted a picture on You-chat of Michael in his Speedos, which, apparently, are crazily unacceptable in America, unless you're swimming for the Olympics. **Hey @roisinkdoyle's brother—YOUR IN AMERICA NOW.** Zara included blinky American flags over Michael's eyes and a red X over his trunks.

I stared at Michael. How was he smiling? I flung the covers back over my head.

"Come on, Ro, it *is* kind of funny. Though she should learn to use an apostrophe. This is that girl you were on about, right?"

If he knew what that girl had done to me—how I'd spent the night reliving it, in nightmares that woke me every few hours—he wouldn't be smiling. "She's not a girl, she's a virus," I murmured into the white fluff muffling my face. My sour breath seeped back at me. Ugh, I hadn't even brushed my teeth before bed.

Michael sat on my bed and tugged the covers away. He frowned at my matted hair, still crunchy from pool water. "C'mere to me now . . ."

"Michael, don't!" He'd gone all Irish. Granny Doyle, Dad's mam, is from Kerry. It's what she says when she's about to lecture us: *"C'mere to me."* Translation: *I'm going to say something you won't like.* Granny is tiny but ferocious as a goose.

"What would Granny Doyle say about Zara Tucci?" Michael asked, reading my mind. "*'That one's a dose,'* she'd say. *'Don't mind her.'*" He didn't get it: You can't ignore a virus. It keeps on, until there's nothing left of you. But Michael nudged me. "Go on, what would she call Zara?"

"A toe-rag." I imagined Granny Doyle as a goose, pecking at Zara till she disappears.

Michael nodded. "I'm only saying: SATs, workaholic parents, global warming . . . these are things. Zara is not a thing." He threw his phone into the air, caught it with the other hand. "It's *my* picture on You-chat, Ro. If I can laugh at it, you can."

I couldn't. The weekend was a nightmare of posts and tags, first about Michael and his snug trunks, then bouncing back on me. Zara said the Irish don't know how to wear clothes, and everyone else piled on. I didn't even know these people. They had avatars instead of pics. Maybe they weren't real people. Zara might have a network of bot trolls, just for me: more fakery, like her messages meant to stop me and Lily becoming friends. I pictured Zara as fake, inside and out: If you unzipped her skin, there'd be no blood, just thousands of robots skittering over one another on clicky legs.

The engine rumbles, and the school bus drops down a gear. We curve around a sharp turn onto yet another highway. Where is this museum, the end of the world? My bag slides away and clunks to the floor. I lunge for it, suddenly sure someone will grab it and make a game of keeping it from me. This is me now: a weakling from a bad teen movie, two scenes away from getting dumped into a garbage bin.

But I was right. A girl is reaching for my bag. She straightens up, the straps hooked over her strong arm. My pulse races as I recognize the black ponytail, the long face. It's the silent girl, the one who helped Mara hold me in the bathroom. Nita. She hands me the bag and flashes a closed-mouth smile that shows her dimples.

I shoot her a death look. Her smile drops and she looks hurriedly at her phone, back to her tunes. Earbud cords hang bright white down the sides of her face. *Yeah, you better look away.* Okay, she was the one who let me go . . . but still. I've never even spoken to her. I can't remember her speaking to anyone, ever. So why did she attack me?

What happened in the bathroom surges back again, stronger now. I pull in a breath, trying to remember what Haley said: They're nothing. I'm strong. Don't let them beat me.

But my hands are trembling. I clamp them between my knees. *Weakling.* I close my eyes and see Zara: She paces toward me. She's going to yank up my dress.

"Isabella Stewart Gardner Museum!" I open my eyes. Mr. Morrison has popped up like a meerkat at the front of the bus, but no one looks at him. Everyone's got their noses to the windows, looking for skyscrapers. Even I know we're in the wrong part of Boston for that. Here it's mostly trees and gray-stone buildings that look like courthouses.

Someone jokes about watching for muggers. Another boy says he heard someone got stabbed near

Fenway last weekend. The bus goes quiet. I see Mara and Zara zip phones carefully into bags. A nervy energy ripples through everyone, more than the day-off buzz of a field trip.

Outside the bus, everyone clusters around Mr. Morrison like baby ducks. Look at their faces! It's suddenly obvious that most of them have never even been into Boston. I bet not one of them could've done what I did: take the train by themselves, find a pool, deal with a lost wallet. I get a surge of satisfaction, remembering the cash still in my purse from Jors.

It's like a little light switches on inside me: not enough to beat back all the dark, but it's something. I'm more of a city kid than any of them. Back in Dublin, I've swum a million times at the Townsend Street pool, surrounded by trams and tourists and exhaust. I didn't think twice about diving straight into Lowell. None of these kids would've had the guts.

Then I catch sight of Zara: She's showing her wrist to Lily, asking if she should zip her fancy watch into her bag, for safety. Lily shakes her head, showing her matching watch; she's keeping hers on.

Zara grips her bag, her eyes darting around for,

I guess, armed muggers. Mara hisses something, and Zara looks: A woman begs for change at the bus stop. My heart goes out to the lady—stained T-shirt, criss-cross scars up her arms—but Zara looks sick, like if the criminals don't get her, the homeless will. Zara only budges when the boy behind shoves her for holding up the queue.

She's mocked me nonstop, telling everyone how pitiful I am. Who's pitiful now?

That light inside me glows brighter. I slip out my phone.

Hales! U should see Zara here: I think being in the city is her worst nightmare. It's like she's panicking. She's PATHETIC.

Ha! Haley shoots back. **That's one we didn't think of: Zara goes to Boston, is mauled by pigeon.**

Ha, perfect! I stuff my phone back in my pocket as we traipse into the museum.

The instant we get inside, Zara flies out of my brain because of the incredible scene in front of me. It's a garden inside the building: a bright courtyard that's flooded with sunlight pouring through the glass roof. We all just gape at the grass and shrubs and actual trees, with marble statues dotted around. An ivy-covered fountain splashes at one end, like something from a dream. Above us, balconies surround the court-yard on all sides, four stories high, all of them carved stone, like an old church. It's so lovely, so European, my heart flies, right up to the orange flowers that cascade like waterfalls from the balconies.

They split us into two groups, and my group gets to go upstairs first. The guide walks us through dim galleries stuffed with art, and I am into it. It's like my brain was dulled by everything, but now it's awake and hungry. I love it all: the paintings and carved furniture and stained glass, the smells of polish and old wood.

The tour guide has to tell Zara and Mara—twice—to stay with the group, because they keep disappearing to go take selfies, slipping under ropes to pose at the balconies. He says if he has to warn them again, he'll have to take our tour back to the lobby.

If she and Mara get us booted from here, I will personally end them. I blast them a don't-you-dare look, though Zara and Mara only have eyes for their phones.

I dash another message to Haley. **omg have u ever been to the Gardner museum in Boston? It is totally FAB.**

the devil twins are trying to get us kicked out though, being idiotic.

They are pathetic, Haley says.

I jam my phone back into my jeans. My eyes go to Zara again and I feel my jaw grind. It's strange. Seeing her so skittish in the city has shrunk her in my mind. She doesn't seem like a virus to me now, or a machine: just a stupid human who's afraid of homeless people.

A stupid human who had two girls hold me down and tried to pull up my dress.

Zara's slipped away to pose on another balcony. She shakes her dark hair in front of her eyes to look tousled for TokTalk or You-chat or whatever, that careful version of perfection she shows her followers. But I know the real Zara: so insecure about Lily, she lied to her and faked those messages to stop Lily becoming friends with me. My fists clench so hard, my nails stab my palms. It's like all my sadness from the weekend has changed to something else, something with teeth and claws.

The guide brings us up more stairs, to a room with big balconies overlooking the courtyard. A huge portrait of Isabella Stewart Gardner stands over us in a gold frame. She looks thoroughly awesome: floor-length black gown, belt of pearls, monster ruby at her throat. The guide tells us Isabella collected everything in the museum herself.

"She inherited millions and spent it all collecting art, building this place—and picking up a few things for herself." He taps a scrapbook full of newspaper cuttings. "Isabella once went to a dance wearing two huge diamonds on her head, the size of walnuts"—he waggles his fingers over his head—"attached to wires, so they moved like antennae and sparkled in the light."

Most people laugh, but I get closer to see the cutting: It's a sketch of Isabella from behind, bare-backed in a gown, giant diamonds bobbing over her head.

"Weirdo." Zara cuts her eyes at me, and Mara giggles. "Friend of yours? Oh, wait. You don't have any."

This time, it's no stress to look Zara in the face.

"Is that the best you've got?" I say, loud enough for everyone to hear. "And who should I be friends with—you? A liar and a fake? No, thanks."

‹ CHAPTER 9 ›

If I live to be a thousand, I won't see anything sweeter than the shock on Zara's face. Her mouth hangs down, like I'm a dog who's suddenly learned to talk. Like it never occurred to her I might bite.

Two boys bust out laughing. "Burned!" one of them says. Our tour guide shakes his head and waves us on to the next room.

Zara's cheeks go red, and Mara presses her skinny lips so tight, they vanish. Only half the class follows the tour guide out; the others linger to watch us. The air crackles, like something's coming. Zara tries to stare me down, but she looks away first, her eyes flicking to the door. She wants to leave, but I'm in the way.

Satisfaction pours through me, like my blood is

made of it. Let her see how it feels, having no escape.

Whip-fast, Zara grabs my phone from my jeans pocket. "You want it?" She backs off and holds it behind her. "Say sorry."

The others *oooooh*, but I barely hear: There's a roar in my ears, and something goes *pop* in my brain. The monster in my chest bursts free, teeth and claws out. I march at Zara.

"GIVE IT," I spit, and Zara's smirk wobbles. This close up, it's obvious how much taller I am.

I lunge for Zara's arm, but she twists away and is at the balcony in an instant. Someone gasps as Zara dangles my phone over the edge.

My first thought is of Haley: Without her, I'm lost. The splash of the fountain sounds below us. If the fall doesn't kill my phone, the water will.

I cross to Zara in two steps. Then her hair is in my fist, and I drag her back from the balcony. She wails in pain, and I catch my phone as she drops it, but her cry cuts through me.

I back away, and Zara does the same, swiping her eyes. Loose hairs are caught in the sweat of my fingers. I become aware of whoops and laughter.

"Told you—fighting Irish," someone says.

My breathing slows. I scrub my hand against my jeans, but Zara's hairs stay trapped. I feel like I'm going to be sick.

"I lost half my tour!" The guide pops his head back into the room, just in time to see Zara rush to a corner with an ancient EXIT sign, Mara following.

"Not that way, girls!" the tour guide calls. "It's under construction back there."

He winces and jogs to where Zara tugs on a door. She mutters that she needs the toilet. The door alarm *beep-beeps* a high whine. The guide says something into his earpiece, and the sound stops. He presses his palm against a control panel in the wall, and it *boops* as the alarm resets. He points Zara and Mara to the other doors and a sign for the bathrooms, and herds the rest of us in the same direction.

"No harm done." He smiles and leads us into a long corridor, making sure we follow this time.

No harm done.

That's not how I feel. I take out my phone, but my hand shakes too much to tell Haley. What would I say, anyway? *"Hey, I hurt Zara! Yay, me!"*

My stomach twists. I don't know how I feel. I can hear whispers hissing around me already, and I'm not even trying: *psycho* and *Irish*. I keep my eyes down. My heart still pounds. I can imagine Michael, asking did I make any friends today. No, Michael, I did the complete, absolute opposite. Because that's me: smoke and ash.

"It is . . . okay." For an instant I think the voice is Lily's, but she's in the downstairs group with Nikesh. I look up to see Nita, peering at me with what I think is sympathy. I still have no idea why she helped Zara attack me. But I haven't seen them together since. She tugs out her earbuds and walks with me. "You feel bad?"

I nod. My face must show it: It's crazy, but I *do* feel bad for grabbing Zara.

Nita shakes her head and makes a face like something stinks. "She is no good."

Well, yeah. My arms curl around my middle. Two chairs stand in the corridor where the guide has stopped us to talk about tapestries. I sink down and Nita sits, too.

"So why'd you help her, then?" I glare at Nita. "Why'd you hold me down, in the girls' bathroom?"

Nita blinks, then looks around. She points to a sign

for the ladies' room: It's where Mara and Zara have vanished to. "Bathroom?"

I huff. How does she not get this? "No." I pretend to yank my own arm. "You held me, in the bathroom." Then I remember the rumors that went around, that I'd tried to fight Zara. My mouth goes dry. "Hang on. Did Zara tell you I was dangerous? That I was going to hurt her?"

Nita's whole face changes as she suddenly understands. Her eyes drop to her shoes. "Yes. Zara says you are dangerous. Asks me to help. To protect. I believe her. Then, I see what she will do to you, so I leave." Nita sighs a long breath; this is a huge speech. For the first time I hear her accent, thick and heavy. She shows me her phone. "Sorry. I only speak a little English."

Now I feel stupid. Nita wasn't listening to music. On her screen is an app, translating words into English from a language I don't recognize. "Is that . . . What is that? It's not Spanish."

"Tzotzil. Mayan language. From Guatemala. I don't speak Spanish."

"Oh, that's . . ." I stare at the portraits, the tapestries—anywhere but at Nita. I think of Lily's mum, how it never occurred to me that people from Japan could be any race. I had no clue there were people in Guatemala who didn't speak Spanish. I thought I had it tough, being new to America, but I'm an idiot; being white and speaking English has probably made things a breeze for me, compared to Nita. No wonder she seems a bit of a loner. Even if she spoke Spanish, she'd have things easier: It's everywhere.

I get this feeling—like I've gotten everything and everyone wrong. And I want to make it right. I'm about to ask Nita if she wants to meet up sometime when someone grips my shoulder.

"Volunteers! Thank you." The tour guide looks stressed. At his side is a girl from our class with a full-on nosebleed, head back and blood on her hands. He finishes saying something into his earpiece and nods at us. "I need two helpers right now. Those selfie girls from your class went to the bathroom but haven't come back. Fetch them for me, please. I need to stay with this pupil till your teacher gets upstairs." He taps his earpiece like he's listening. "Yep, third floor," he says. *"Thank you,"* he mouths to us, and turns away, so there's no arguing.

Brilliant. Fetching Zara is not what I need right now. Or ever. I drag myself off the chair. Nita rolls her eyes and heads back down the corridor to the room with Isabella's portrait, while I go the other way.

I saw Zara skulk back from the bathroom and have an idea where she might be now. The museum is a series of rooms and wide corridors across four levels, all with windows and balconies overlooking the garden courtyard. Zara and Mara keep doing this stupid thing where they take pictures of each other on balconies, across the open space in the middle. There's one balcony that's framed by crazy-long flowers that hang down from upstairs: perfect for a selfie that lets them pretend they're in an Italian villa.

I spot Zara at the end of the corridor and jog toward her. "The guide says come back. Now!"

She throws me a look. She's headed for a door that says NO ADMITTANCE, but she tugs it open and sails through, like rules aren't for her. "Ooh, you gonna make me?"

I blow out a breath. Anyone else could've been sent to fetch her. I'm obviously cursed. I follow Zara into what looks like a gloomy living room. Gilded wood panels glint in the darkness, but most surfaces are draped with sheets, and ladders and toolboxes are dotted about. We're definitely not supposed to be in here.

I spot Zara and nearly choke. "Are you mad? Get away from those!"

She's unlatching the glass shutters that cover over the balcony. Some of the balconies have these floor-to-ceiling doors that the tour guide told us to leave alone. Outside, the orange flowers trail down, framing a distant view of our group at the windows opposite. I can see Nita with Mara, who's holding her phone and waving at Zara to come out and pose.

"Piss off, Roisin. Isn't that what ye Irish say?"

I pull Zara's arm, one last attempt to bring her back, but she snatches it away. "Don't touch me!" she yells, loud enough to wake the dead.

"Fine." I am done. Let them send someone else to deal with Zara's mess. Being near her makes me want to scratch my skin off. Sun still lights the courtyard outside. I'm going back for a last look before Zara gets us kicked out.

Zara flings open the glass shutters and steps onto the balcony.

Then time goes strange because it must take just a second, but I see details: the stone dust, the sandpaper, even the kneepads someone left in front of the half-repaired balcony, with its partial railing and the gap that Zara walks straight through—like Michael used to do, when he'd pretend not to see the pool and walk into the deep end, then gasp and splutter in fake shock.

This shock is real, and the screams, too—Zara's screams—as she twists and grabs at the air, catching only flowers. There are shrieks of "No!" and someone says, "Don't look," but we all look at Zara, below us in the courtyard, a crooked shape on the white tiles, the green grass, and a spreading pool of red.

‹ CHAPTER 10 ›

It must have crossed your mind. That she had it coming, I mean.

I shake my head, though Haley can't see. **It was just . . . so real. If you had seen her. The blood.**

I stop typing and rub my eyes. I was dying to tell Haley about the museum, but she's being . . . I don't know. Weird. When our bus finally got back to Eastborough, Mum and Michael were all over me, demanding details. Dad even rang, though it was the middle of the night in Dublin by then. But I couldn't face going into it with them. I gave them the barest info and slipped away to plug in my phone so I could tell Haley instead: the panic and screaming and how calm the museum people and the paramedics were, making sure we weren't traumatized by what we'd seen. Mara and Lily both went in the ambulance with Zara. Mr. Morrison was so happy Zara was alive, I think he would've agreed to anything.

But she was a monster to u, Ro. I think it's the universe giving her what she deserved.

I shudder, remembering the impossible angle of Zara's twisted leg on the ground. One of the huge tree-fern things broke her fall. It saved her life, the paramedics said. **She's super lucky she didn't smash her head open**, I write.

Too bad she didn't. Drip, drip, dead. Nobody would miss her.

I blink at my phone.

JK, Haley adds, when I don't reply. Then winky face, crying laughing, love heart.

There's a soft knock, and my bedroom door opens. A pile of folded laundry, followed by my mother. She frowns at my phone, plucking it out of my hand and powering it off in one smooth movement. "It's late, sweetheart." She opens a drawer, puts the laundry inside, and sits on my bed, all of which is so unusual, I know she's freaked out. I'm too shattered to say she's the last person who should lecture anyone about being up late. "Do you want to talk about it now?"

I give a groan that I hope will make her give up, but she rests a hand on my leg. She used to do this when I was little: I'd make her leave her hand on my knee or my shoulder till I fell asleep. I roll over and look at her.

"Remember Seamus Dowling?"

Mum nods in the darkness. "Snotty kid." He was, too. He lived in the farm opposite Granny Doyle's in Kerry, and he had a permanent wet lip from a nose that streamed constantly. He was always showing off, I think because we were from Dublin. "It was like that time with the fork." Seamus nearly killed himself and all of us one summer, daring us to jump off things in the barn, till he landed on a pitchfork. He didn't die, but I'd never seen so much blood.

"Oh, yes. Sorry, darling." Mum rubs my knee. "The stuff of bad dreams." She pauses. "That poor girl. I suppose you want to talk it over with the others who saw it, but keep this off." She puts my phone on the dresser.

I don't tell Mum that Haley didn't see the accident; she just wishes she had. I hate that she's being so brutal about this. Haley's the only person who knows my whole ugly saga with Zara, including the fact that my brain still wakes me in the night, reliving that instant when she was about to pull up my dress. But then Zara nearly died. So it's like I'm not allowed to hate her now. Because what would that make me? I need to sort out how I feel. But I don't think Haley can help.

"Mum."

"Yes?" she says, when I don't say anything more. But how can I put it into words?

"The girl who fell—she was horrible. To me."

"*O-kay.*" Mum stretches the word, like she's not sure she wants to hear what's next. Like I might be about to confess I pushed Zara.

"But I don't feel glad or yay or anything. Should I?"

"Oh!" I can hear the relief in her voice. Wow. Thanks, Mum. Though, for all she's seen me in the last few months, I could've turned into a murderer and she wouldn't know. But then Mum sits closer and puts her hand against my cheek, and all I want is for her to keep it there forever. "Darling. Of course you shouldn't be glad. You're a human being."

She kisses my head, which I'm way too old for but

which seems okay at two a.m., in the dark. Her cheek leans against my hair, and the smell of her face cream makes my heart well up. I should tell her everything. I used to: updating her on my day, my classes, my friends. But she's missed too much. And my problems aren't kid-sized anymore.

She stands up and I realize she's brought me FRED. She's holding it under one arm, its black tail drooping down. "Do you want me to . . . ?" She gestures that she can tuck it in with me, if I'd like. I would not like. How can she not know how freaky that thing is? She nods. "Right, then. Get some sleep, sweetheart."

Sleep doesn't come. I can see my phone, the black screen reflecting the moonlight. I should switch it on again and say good night to Haley; she'll think I'm cross with her. After Lily's party, though, when I went back onto You-chat after Mum said phones off, Jeeves turned me in. He called out a warning, and he must have told Mum, because she thumped the wall between our bedrooms with a muffled but specific threat about taking my phone. I must be the only person in the world whose mother uses robot overlords to enforce her rules.

Wait—not the only person.

I sit up, my insides squirming, remembering Lily. I can still see her, sitting in the ambulance, the knees of her white jeans soaked red where she'd kneeled next to Zara. She and Nikesh were with the tour on the ground floor, and Lily was right there, just after it happened. She yelled into her watch, probably to get her Jeeves to call an ambulance, and peeled off her cardigan to cover Zara. The rest of us froze, as helpful as the marble statue that Zara had missed by centimeters.

I kick off the covers, writing the message to Lily in my head as my phone powers up. If it's a normal text instead of You-chat, maybe Jeeves won't tell on me. **You were brilliant at the museum,** I type super fast. **It's awful about Zara. Talk tomorrow?**

I hit send, then hover over the You-chat icon. Maybe I can send Haley a quick message. But my thumb hits the power button instead.

No one can concentrate on classes today, and by nine thirty our Geometry teacher has put seven phones in jail, a pink cardboard box on his desk. Zara is dead by midmorning, alive again by lunch, and paralyzed by fifth period, according to You-chat, where the comments under Mara's post—a photo of Zara on a stretcher, being wheeled into Mass General—now have 157 versions of the truth.

You-chat is giving me an utter breakdown, but it's hard to look away. By last period, people have started asking who was there when Zara fell, did someone push her.

@roisinkdoyle wuz there. I SAW her grab Zara, Mara says.

> Irish girl? The one who said she'd rip @zara_xx_oo's head off?

> Y, it was right after she beat Zara down to get her phone back.

I did not beat Zara down! I stopped her from chucking my phone over the balcony!

I try to breathe, but it's like something is crushing me. This is SO UNFAIR, I could burn the world. It was Zara who bullied me, every day, no mercy. But the instant I reacted, she turned it around, getting me banned from TokTalk, making people think I was unstable.

And now this. The museum. Our fight, then her crazy accident.

At least Lily believes that Zara's fall wasn't my fault. Things are, weirdly, good with us. She told me to stay off You-chat, so we've been texting. The true story—I heard from Lily—is that Zara shattered her leg and was in surgery all night but should recover. Mara went home, but Lily's still at the hospital—Mr. Morrison, too. Lily says he's walking around like a guilt zombie: He says he should've stayed with our half of the tour.

No one's going to blame him, I type. I'm in the loos again, sitting on the shelf by the sinks.

Guess not, Lily answers. **The museum shouldn't have left the balcony half-fixed, or made it so easy for anyone to get into that room. I heard Zara just walked right in there.**

I frown, remembering the tour guide. He used his palm print to secure that old exit Zara tried to use. It makes no sense that Zara sailed right through the NO ADMITTANCE door into the room that was under construction. **It is weird that we were both able to get into** there. The guide said the museum had a huge theft years ago, so the security they use now is super high-tech. But the door wasn't even locked.

Roisin . . . I'm sorry.

Do you have to go? Maybe she's supposed to be at Zara's bedside, giving her sips of water or whatever.

No, I mean—at the party. When you told me what Zara did to you. In the bathroom. I said the wrong thing, didn't I?

I push out a breath. It feels so good to hear that, at last. **It's fine,** I type back to Lily. **I took you by surprise. Myself, too. Didn't mean to tell u.**

I'm glad you did! You've got to tell a teacher, too. No one should be attacked like that.

Lily's right. I look around the bathroom, with its slippy floor. It happened right here. I won't forgive Zara. I can't. I swallow hard. **Zara was horrible to me,** I type. **But I feel awful that she's hurt. It's complicated.**

I scrub my forehead. Lily will think I'm a monster. If only I could talk to Haley about this. But she's acting like she's glad Zara's suffering—maybe because she's not totally over that horrible girl, Coral. These mean girls: They really mess with your head.

I get it, Lily says. I talked to Zara on Saturday, after that stupid post about your brother. She owes you a big apology, for everything. It's just—she's not even conscious right now.

The bell screams suddenly, and I jump off the shelf. I text Lily that I've gtg and dive into the corridor crush, pushing my way back to Art for my bag. The substitute teacher gives me an earful for disappearing for twenty minutes, and I mutter an apology, but I'm not even looking at her, I'm making myself check You-chat and Haley's messages. There are loads.

U there?

Ro, msg me when you get this

Hello, are you dead?

Either her teachers in Maine don't care who's on their phone, or Hales is good at hiding hers, because the timestamps are all through the day, when she's obvs in class.

When I reach the bus, I flop into the front seat and dash her a message. **Haley, SORRY, loads of drama today. How r you?**

I don't wait for her answer but flick through other stuff I've missed. A text from Mum, to say she's thinking of me. Which is nice. One from Dad, too. Seems like they're glad it wasn't their daughter who fell off a balcony.

My phone rings. Unrecognized number. For an instant, I wonder if it's Haley, but Jeeves's familiar voice sounds in my earbuds. *"It's a call from Jors Kuypers, a contact from You-chat. Should I put it through?"*

I say okay, and Jors's face and floppy blond fringe appear. "Good afternoon, Roisin! How would you like some good news about de study?"

The what? Slowly, my brain catches up. I haven't thought about Jors or my random trip to City University of Lowell since things got so crazy. "Sure, go on."

"Okay! I am sending you your voucher for the part two, and we're doubling it to one hundred twenty dollars, because your usage levels are nice and high—about six hundred megabytes a day. Good job!"

You-chat, right. Something about tracking my usage and my mood. Wait—did he say one hundred twenty dollars? Whoa. I can buy another couple outfits and new makeup; my eyebrow pencil is a scratchy stub.

"Ah, but—you weren't on the app today very much." Jors looks like he's waiting for an explanation. I almost laugh. *"Hey, use your phone more."* It's the opposite of what every other adult says.

"Is that a problem?" I ask.

He tilts his head in a way that could mean *maybe.* "It's a learning algorithm, it needs de data, so—yes. Your usage today is"—he looks down—"almost zero. So. I call to check is anything wrong."

I don't know what to say, and the bus is slowing for my stop. I grab my bags and stand up. "I need to run, sorry."

Jors gives a don't-worry wave. He says he'll send me the payment and tells me to keep up the good work.

As I climb our hill, what he said niggles at me. Is that what I'm doing—working for Jors? I'm mentally spending his money already, mostly on M·A·C. But I can't shake the feeling that something is off. Everything feels off today: not chatting to Haley, and Jors pushing me to use You-chat, and the image my brain keeps flashing of Zara falling. I can't grasp what's wrong, but it's like I can smell it, like a whiff of smoke in the house.

I shiver and realize that actual smoke drifts from our neighbor's chimney. More freak Massachusetts weather. I zip my hoodie. The temperature's dropped fifteen degrees. Dad couldn't cope with the weather when he first lived here, either; he met Mum when they were students at Harvard, in a snowstorm. Dad had no winter coat, because he was too Irish to think he'd need one. I can get Dad a proper birthday present now, thanks to Jors.

I sigh and open You-chat again. Jors is right; I've hardly looked at it today. And I've left Haley hanging. She's typing another message as I watch—about a boy who sits behind her in Chemistry.

Good looking? I type.

Haley gives me a shrug emoji. **Kinda. He's nice and he makes me laugh.** She pauses. **It's good to talk to u. Missed u today.** She adds a teardrop face.

I'm the worst friend. Haley's been so supportive, and now I'm avoiding her, just because she's a bit hardcore about Zara. I scan her other messages: She must've thought I ghosted her. Sorry, sorry, sorry, Haley. After all she's been through with Coral, I don't want her to think I'm abandoning her. I read everything I've missed, but keep zipping back to the live chat, so she'll know I'm listening.

I want to ask him to the Memorial Day dance. Would that be weird?

Go for it, I type. **You don't get what you want in life by sitting around hoping.** I scroll back farther, to be sure I've seen all her messages, and my heart just about stops.

A rock should fall from space and flatten her in her bed.

SHE should fall from space

Into boiling oil.

Or sharks. Sharks are always good.

My breath catches in my chest. I'm shaking as I flick back to Mara's picture of Zara at the hospital.

Panic climbs my throat as I scan the latest comments. Mara keeps saying she saw me grab Zara, right before she fell. Lily tells them they're being insane, and even Nita pipes up to say she watched the whole thing, and I was nowhere near Zara when it happened.

Well the cops wanna talk to everyone, Mara says. **That's what I heard.**

Good, someone says. **They can go all LAW AND ORDER on her butt.**

It's like someone's punched through my chest and grabbed my heart. I stop to lean against the oak tree. I scroll frantically through the stream, but there's no more mention of cops. I pray Mara's making that up. But everyone's heard the stories: bullied kids try to kill themselves, and then police find the cruel stuff people said to them online. If they investigate Zara's accident, they'll see I promised to tear her head off. They could demand all my DMs, too—even the jokey messages about Zara dying.

Falling and dying.

I jump as the phone buzzes again. **Good thinking. I think I will ask him to the dance. See? U are awesome.**

I don't tell my thumb to do it, but I press, hold, delete each Zara revenge-fantasy message I sent Haley. My heart gallops like fury. Now there's a weird one-sided conversation with just Haley's messages, because I can only erase my own. Unfortunately.

I stumble toward our house.

"Mission Control to Roisin. Come in, Roisin." Michael hisses pretend-static into his fist. He stands in our doorway, grinning. He drops the NASA voice. "You've got a face like a funeral. Cheer up! We're going to another par-tay." He waves his phone. "Hiro said his dad's arranged to take us all to Maine for Memorial Day weekend, because the mother-units have to work. Their family has a holiday house in someplace called"—he checks his screen—"Old Orchard Beach. Ever heard of it?"

‹ CHAPTER 11 ›

stare at Michael. A hundred thoughts rip through me. Haley lives in Old Orchard Beach. I have to meet her. Warn her. God, I don't even know what I'll say. But every fiber in me screams that Haley and I both need to erase these messages about Zara now, before we get hauled into some police station, like every American cop show I've ever seen. I can't text Haley about this; that would only leave more messages, all about the same thing . . . we wanted Zara to suffer. A lot.

"Yes. Okay. Good," I stammer, and nudge past Michael up the stairs to our flat.

He follows me. "Do you mean actual good, or, 'Good, it's just a flesh wound'? Because you look awful."

"Thanks a million."

Michael is still behind me when I shut my bedroom door in his face. "Okay!" he calls. "Good chat!"

I don't have brain space even to be annoyed with his chronic cheeriness. But, oh, to be Michael. My round room lets me pace without stopping, but I'm soon dizzy and sick with it, or maybe it's the guilt, which is drowning me now—even though *I didn't do a thing to Zara.*

Hales, I type, and hesitate. How in the world do I say this? **YOU WILL NEVER GUESS where I'm going this weekend.**

Paris? Tokyo? The Moon? She sends an Eiffel Tower emoji, sushi, a crescent moon.

I laugh. All places she knows I'm dying to visit.

Old Orchard Beach!!!!

I stare at my screen, waiting for the fireworks and party hats. There's a pause.

But you dont have a car.

This is still true. Eastborough is filled with kids whose parents have holiday homes in New Hampshire or Cape Cod or wherever. They pile into their giant cars and roar up the motorway every weekend to hang out somewhere better. Michael and I mostly sit around like car-less losers.

Lily's dad is driving. They have a place at the beach. Check it! I flip back to Lily's timeline on You-chat, to the beachy pics I liked way back when. I can't believe I'm going to stay there. I ping Haley the link. I'm still waiting for her *yay!* It doesn't come.

LILY? Ro. Lily's queen of mean. WHAT R U DOING?

I shake my head. Haley doesn't see how decent Lily's been. I've already told Haley I made a mistake: Lily wasn't the one who canceled our plans when I first got here, it was loopy Zara, sending fake messages from Lily's phone. But Haley seems to like Lily less and less. This is jealousy, I'm sure of it.

She's nice, Hales, really. But listen—you know you're my bestie, right? We haven't said that yet to each other, but now feels like the right time.

For real? Haley includes hearts and stars. **Because ur mine, too.**

I smile. **Come on, this will be awesome. What's good to do in Old Orchard Beach?**

We trade messages about cool stuff to do, like the funfair rides and something called a clam roll, which sounds revolting, but I'll try it. Haley sounds like a guidebook; she obviously loves the place. **Stick with me,** she says. **Vacationers like your little friend don't know the best parts of OOB.**

Haley's like this all week. More digs at Lily, who she insists is fake. It's horrible, feeling torn between them.

Lily is psyched about the trip. Zara is recovering quickly, so that worry's off her mind. She really wanted our mums to come, but they're doing something critical at the lab, even though Memorial Day is apparently some sacred American barbecue weekend when no one works. Hiro and Michael keep texting about their plans for the beach. I'm the only one who's all conflicted.

I haven't told Lily I'm seeing Haley. Mixing friends never works. And I couldn't trust Haley not to be super rude, if they did meet. I obviously haven't told Haley we need to delete those messages on her phone, either, or that police might be getting involved. I'll say it when I see her: We're meeting at the school dance, where Haley's invited that boy from her Chem class. Between Lily and Haley, my head is mush, trying to remember what secrets I'm keeping from each of them.

But that weirdness is nothing compared to the

nightmare school has become. Nobody's been contacted by the police—yet—but I've become the punching bag. Between classes I keep my eyes on the ground, but it's hard to ignore what everyone's saying, to my face and on You-chat: I'm a crazy Irish assassin who's obsessed with Zara. I threatened her once and probably did it again, scaring Zara into falling off the balcony.

Lily says to ignore them, and they'll be gossiping about something different tomorrow, but she's not the one getting *PSYCHO* notes in her locker (someone has learned how to spell it).

And then there's Mara. She roams the halls like she's recently widowed, pale and shocked, stopping to accept sympathy or trade information about Zara's recovery in exchange for big-eyed hugs. I try to arrange my face in an expression that says, *I'm genuinely freaked by what happened and am definitely not hiding any morbid jokes about Zara dying.* If anyone knew about the messages Haley and I sent, we'd be arrested. I'm sure of it.

My nerves are shot, and by Wednesday I'm in floods of tears after History; my horrible teacher will fail me if I don't give her my World War II project outline by the end of the day. Huddling in the loos again, I write to

Haley. I haven't messaged her much today—her anti-Lily rants are stressing me out—but I need a Haley pep talk now. I'm becoming the worst kind of friend, the kind who dumps on you when they're down and ignores you the rest of the time. But Haley isn't mad; she even offers to help, saying she just did World War II in her school.

An hour later, my phone buzzes, and I can't believe what I'm looking at: Haley's sent a list of everything I should cover in my report on Pearl Harbor. It's utterly perfect—I can just hand this in as my outline. **Tysm!!! I don't deserve u**, I say, swallowing down tears.

No bother, she answers, and I smile; she's sounding Irish again. **It's what friends do. And hey! I can't wait to see u!**

By the time we're piled into Mr. Tanaka's Lexus SUV on Friday afternoon, flying up Interstate 95 to Maine, I still haven't told Lily my plans. Hiro and Michael are like giddy six-year-olds, punching each other in the arms as part of some highway game. Lily's up front with her dad, so it's just me and my guilt in the back, watching the boys mess about, avoiding my phone.

I squirm in my seat. I must be the only person who's ever been uncomfortable in this much leathery luxury. Lily has been so nice, but I can't possibly tell her about seeing Haley. *I need to get my best friend to delete the messages about wanting* your *best friend to die, if that's cool with you?* I'm rubbish at lying. If I tell Lily anything, I'll spill everything. No. The only way is to keep my mouth closed and slip out of the house tonight, somehow.

Haley knows I'm meeting her at her school's dance but not why. I am so excited to finally hang out with her. She's been my north, south, east, and west through the whole Zara drama. She realized that her hard-core comments about Zara's accident freaked me out, and she hasn't said anything else like that. What she has done, though, is all these little kindnesses that only a best friend who really knows you would think of. There was another one this morning: an easy pasta recipe with chili and garlic that Haley found; she knows Mum's never around to cook.

The SUV finally pulls off the highway and weaves through streets of blocky wooden houses. Old Orchard Beach looks like Eastborough, but more basic: not many houses have gardens, giving the place a city-center feel, though it's a small town. Mr. Tanaka parks outside a two-story shack that looks like a stiff breeze could blow it down.

Hiro and Michael have reached peak toddler mode: Michael snatches Hiro's baseball cap and races to the door. The tang of sea hits the back of my throat: I think of last summer and language camp in Connemara, stumbling around trying to ask for Cokes and sweets at the shops in our basic Irish. There's another smell of home, too.

"Am I smelling chips? Fries, I mean?" I follow Lily toward the shack, which I realize isn't the holiday home, as I'd stupidly thought, but a restaurant. My tummy creases with hunger and I sniff at the fried air.

Lily stretches toward the watery-blue sky, then rests an arm around my shoulder. "I literally dream about this place."

"Best fish and chips in the world." Mr. Tanaka grins and gestures me through the door.

"And OH-migod, the lobster rolls?" Hiro calls back to us, putting on a fake teen-girl voice that makes Michael laugh. He sits at a picnic table by a window that looks onto a tangle of metal arches. It takes my brain a second to figure out what the strange scaffolding is.

"Is that a *roller coaster*?" Michael's face looks like it's Christmas. "We have to go!" It *is* a roller coaster. This must be the funfair Haley meant. The coaster rises high over an amusement park that's plonked right in the middle of town. It looks like it's filled with classic rides, the kind that swing and fling you around, although they're motionless now.

Hiro nods. "It should open for the season this weekend. The roller coaster's the best, isn't it, Lil?"

Lily laughs. "You get sick on it every time."

"I've got a good feeling about this year." Hiro nods at the waitress, who gives us a super-bright American smile and a friendliness that's genuine, I realize, when she hugs Mr. Tanaka.

I've never tasted lobster in my life, but it's so good: pinky chunks of it burst out of a buttered hot dog bun that's almost too big to hold, and it's tossed in some dressing that is life-changingly delicious, like Hiro promised. The chips taste just like home.

I watch Lily paint circles in her ketchup with a chip, giggling at Michael. There's something more relaxed about her here, like Maine is her happy place. I can't help feeling it, too. Maybe it's the seagulls, or the beach air, or the chilled-out smiles of everyone around, but the tension ebbs out of me. Old Orchard Beach feels like somewhere that good times have seeped right into the floorboards, the memories of a million summer days.

Everyone knows Lily's family. The owner comes to our table, wiping his palms on his apron, to shake Mr. Tanaka's hand. Later, at an ice-cream stand down the road, the lady giving us our cones asks about Lily's mum and quizzes Hiro about college. When I say I feel too stuffed to climb back into the Lexus and ask if we can walk to their holiday house from here, Mr. Tanaka says I'm a genius. He'll pick up groceries, and we can walk to the cottage.

"It's, like, a mile," Hiro groans.

"Dude, you swim, like, eight miles a day," Michael says, and licks a drip of vanilla that creeps down his cone.

Mr. Tanaka claps my back, and I grin. I super love Lily's dad. He seems as pumped to be here as the others. Lily says he's got a painting studio in the cottage, and that we'll hardly see him once he's lost in his watercolors.

The streets are lined with similar wood-shingled houses, with flowerpots and American flags around the doors. A blue line of flat water ahead lets me know we're heading for the beach. I get that sunny, unreal feeling, like that day in Lowell: that this is a scene from an American film—a happily-ever-after, Lily's-America film, rich and sweet. I feel the tiniest bit disloyal to Haley, because we're supposed to do all this together tomorrow—though I'm still not sure what I'll say to Lily. It's bizarre that my only two friends in this country have houses in the same place. It'd be so much easier if we could all just hang out, but something tells me that'll never happen.

"Hold my sundae?" Lily's cup is still warm with hot fudge, and I see melting balls of purple ice cream. She takes a pic as we pass a blue house with tubs of red tulips by the door. Soon we're picking our way down a narrow path through the dunes. She tosses her empty cup into a bin and turns to take another pic from the beach, the blue house just visible.

"Zara's house—old house, I mean."

"Really?" A breeze throws my hair forward onto my mint-chocolate-chip cone. I pinch green goo off a curl and flick it onto the sand. I remember Lily saying Zara had moved to Eastborough from Maine, but I didn't know Zara also came from Old Orchard Beach.

"We met here in second grade. Zara was year-round, but we just came in summer."

We walk on, watching the boys goof on the sand ahead, and the gulls that cry in the sky. But that sun-kissed feeling of being part of something perfect has leaked away. All this should be Zara's, and was: the role of best friend in Lily's Old Orchard Beach movie, with lobster rolls and smiling locals and beach walks to the cottage. I imagine Lily's bedroom here: Is it another shrine of photos to Zara, pre-evil?

Wait! Maybe Zara knows Haley. The thought stops me mid-lick. And, ugh, that mouthful had sand in it. It grinds between my teeth, and I try to spit without Lily seeing. I am redefining classy today. "Can I dump this?" I hold up my cone and wipe my chin. There's no bin nearby, and I don't fancy lobbing it into the waves that break on the shore; I'll be spotted littering and ruin the good Tanaka name.

Lily looks at my sad cone, her mouth to one side in thought. "Give it."

She snaps off the pointy end and plunges the rest of the cone into the sand, then she breaks the handful of sugar cone into pieces that she scatters around us. It's only seconds before a gray-white gull lands with a rush of wings, lunging for the food with its yellow beak. Two more birds ease out of the sky, fold away lanky wings, and race to peck at the melting cone. "Genius," I say, and Lily shrugs.

"My mother calls them sky rats, but I love them." Lily lifts her phone to take a pic of me while I'm surrounded by gulls. I raise my arms like I'm master of birds, and she smiles.

We walk in silence. The wind blows Lily's hair to the side, and she holds her arms around her middle. I'm starting to recognize her uncomfortable-conversation pose. "Zara had a horrible dad," she says. "Not an excuse for how mean she's been to you, but . . ."

"It's fine." It's not fine. But I don't want to talk about Zara. My phone, with the ugly messages about her, feels like it's roaring in my pocket—like the ticking heart under the floorboards, in that story we read in English.

My stomach plunges as I remember there's even more stuff on my phone that I'd hate Lily to see: all the mean "Queen Lily" stuff Haley says. And there's more. **You really think Lily likes u? What if she's laughing at u with Zara behind your back?**

"No, it's not fine, it's just—I don't want to blab about Zara's private stuff." Lily breathes out. "Long story short: Bad dad, moved to Eastborough because we were there, her mom remarried a nice guy, and there's a new baby. And I'm not—we're not—friends like we used to be." Lily says this last part like it's a terrible confession.

I nod. My friend Maisie back home thought she'd love it when her sister was born. But she was so jealous, she wanted to leave the baby on the tram so someone else could take it. If Zara had that baby jealousy going on, and that baggage of an awful dad . . . and then Lily's drifting away to Nikesh, plus she's starting to be friends with me . . .

I let the thought trail off. I'm not about to forgive Zara. Remembering what she did still makes me want to kick something. She didn't just sabotage the friendship between me and Lily, she humiliated me in front of everyone, then she tried to strip me. I haven't slept through the night since. "People change," I murmur.

Lily shakes her head. "We weren't supposed to. We had this Best Friend Code thing." Lily points to some huge rocks rising from the wet sand at the shoreline. "We sat and said it right there. We promised we'd tell each other the truth and always be friends and never get mad."

I can't help thinking of me and Haley. What would our Best Friend Code be? *I promise to make you laugh and help you survive bullies and always be online for you.* "How can you promise never to be mad at someone?" I ask.

"You can't. But we were seven, you know?"

Ahead of us, the boys are heading away from the water, toward a house.

"That's the *cottage*?"

Lily doesn't answer but calls to Hiro, who's shouting for us to hurry. She takes off in a run, and my sandals slide in the sand, but I race to follow and catch up to them at the boardwalk. A long, rope-edged path leads to the house, giving us a good look at it. *Cottage* made me think of Kerry, and the little stone cottages bunched by the side of the road opposite Granny's.

But this is magnificent: blue and huge and right on the beach, its wraparound porch like a skirt around a grand old lady. Sunset has begun to color the sky and sea, and the windows reflect its warm light. One of the upper-floor rooms has a balcony, with white-framed French doors that glow pink; so do the floppy white flower heads of the bushes across the lawn.

Lily tries to squeeze past Hiro, but he's faster and presses his hand to a panel by the door. Lily shouts something in Japanese. Hiro grins and waves a theatrical hand in the air as the door swings open.

"Welcome home, Hiro," says a Jeeves-like voice from somewhere, though I can't see anything like Jeeves's glowing discs. Everything looks old-school: a classic sitting room with flowered upholstery and a brick fireplace. A ceiling fan is still, and wide steps lead upstairs. There's no hint of where the voice is coming from. *"And Lily,"* the voice adds, like an afterthought.

Hiro laughs. "Smart house," Lily says to me. "Mom's idea, obvs, though Hiro—has—to—be—first." She whacks his arm with each word.

A jumble of beeps and notifications buzzes through pockets and bags. "You've been on our house Wi-Fi, so

Taiko recognizes you here, too," Hiro says. Everyone flops onto sofas and chairs to catch up on what they've missed, but I delay looking at my frantically vibrating phone. I've been out of coverage for a while; there are probably a dozen pre-dance-jitters messages from Haley about meeting that boy tonight.

I've got jitters of my own. I've wanted this so long—to hang out with Haley—but what if she doesn't like me when we meet? I have no idea what she'll do when I ask her to delete those messages about Zara. How would I feel if I met my best friend in person for the first time, and they asked me to hand over my phone so they could start erasing things? I don't want to make her cross. And I can't lose her.

My stomach is tight as a fist as I open You-chat, but it's not what I think. It's worse.

Haley's message is a screen capture of the photo Lily posted earlier, of me and the gulls.

Red-faced rage emojis, followed by sobbing faces, surround Haley's words.

Having a fab time in OOB with your BFF, I see. U know what? Don't bother coming to the dance. You obvs don't need me anymore.

< CHAPTER 12 >

You don't have to do that; you're a guest." Lily gives me a pained look, leaning in the doorway of our room, the very beautiful room with the balcony overlooking a now-starry sea. Everything here is as classy as the rest of Lily's life: antique chest of drawers, gorgeously thick rug, old seascape oil paintings—proper art, like in a museum. Another dish of hand-painted birds, like the ones by Lily's front door in Eastborough, nestles on the table between our beds, feathers shining in the lamplight.

"It's fine! Nearly done!" I fling the fitted sheet over my bed. I've been all exclamation marks and this-is-so-great cheer since we got here. My phone, and Haley's jealous message that I haven't answered, are stuffed into the bottom of my backpack.

All through dinner and then Scrabble in front of the fire with Mr. Tanaka—complete with cookies and hot chocolate that Hiro brought in on a tray—I've grinned my way through the evening, counting the minutes until I can sneak out to make things right with Haley. "I need to help out: Your family is totally spoiling us."

"You win. I am just wiped." Lily trudges in, yawning hugely, and falls onto her bed. I slipped up here to make both beds while the others were washing up. I planned to brave my phone, too—tell Haley she's still my bestie, obviously—but I convinced myself I didn't have to. I'll see her at the middle school and say it all then: *Sorry* I upset you, *sorry* for dragging you into the Zara jokes that I'm now desperate to hide, *sorry* if a cop knocks on your door and demands to see your phone.

Jeeves says the school is a long walk away, but if I run, I'll make it. The dance ends at ten, though; I need to go now.

Lily meant what she said about being wiped, because before I've even brushed my teeth, she's snoring. I freeze, unable to believe my luck, then my brain kicks in. I shove my pillows into a me shape, in case Lily wakes up and sees I've gone, although from the sound of her, she's deeply under. The quiet snores are such a human sound, my heart goes out to her: She must be exhausted. She spent two nights at the hospital this week with Zara.

I grab my phone and pad downstairs, through the darkness. Hiro and Michael are watching a movie in their room, but I don't know where Mr. Tanaka is: He vanished into the studio earlier. In the living room, a full moon paints silver rectangles on the floor, and holy mother of God, I nearly scream. A doglike lump creeps over the carpet. My fingernails dig my cheeks where I've clamped my mouth closed, but my panic calms as I stare at the humming shape, with its flashing red light. It's not a dog; it's a robot vacuum, quietly hoovering our cookie crumbs from earlier.

I pull on my shoes, and I'm about to touch the door handle when I spot something: Another red light shines from a control pad on the wall. I remember Taiko, their AI who greeted us. If this is a security alarm, he might wail like mad when the door opens.

"Jeeves," I whisper, hunched over my phone. "I need

to leave the house. Do you know Taiko?" It sounds ludicrous, but maybe they're friends in their creepy AI dimension.

My phone screen goes black and pulses with that heartbeat light that means Jeeves is thinking. I scramble for my earbuds just in time, and his voice sounds in my ears.

"Taiko became operational at the MIT Boston Robotics Lab in Cambridge, Massachusetts, on January twelfth—"

"Jeeves, stop." I clutch my forehead. I don't have time for this. Unless I get out now, I won't catch Haley. "Can you make Taiko open the door?"

Almost before I've finished speaking, the control pad light blinks to green, and the latch clicks softly. The door swings inward, opening a fan of moonlight into the room, and relief floods through me. I slip out, phone clutched to my chest, and I run.

Jeeves, who I deeply love at this instant, murmurs instructions, and my desperation-fueled legs streak me through the streets, past dark houses and the occasional bright window. Moonlight bounces off pickup trucks and turns the American flags black striped.

Closer to town there's more traffic, and the streets

widen. I can feel drivers slow as they pass me, staring. I keep my eyes ahead, breath pounding in my ears. I'm out for a run. A night run. People do this.

"*Turn left.*" I nod at Jeeves's instructions and cut away from the main street. The road ahead is silent with darkness. Yellow light pools under a single, distant streetlamp. This instantly feels like a bad idea.

"Hey! You lost?" I nearly leap out of my skin: Someone in a battered white van has slowed to a crawl next to me. I give a noncommittal wave and throw him a tight smile. He's skinny, maybe Mum's age, and smiles back from behind a scraggled beard. It's not a nice smile: too familiar, like he knows me, and we're friends.

A chill crawls over me. The settled darkness ahead is an impossibility now. I do an about-face, like this was the plan, back toward the lights. A sudden cramp punctures my side. Not now! I clench my teeth and try to push through it, but it's like a knife in my ribs.

There's a squeak of tires that must be the van making a U-turn. As I reach the main road, its grubby shape is next to me again. The van looks like it's been dragged slowly through a scrap heap, with deep gouges across the door.

"*O-kay.*" Jeeves has sensed my change of direction. He uses that judgy tone, like I've messed up, but he'll fix it. "*In two hundred feet, take a left.*"

"You sure you're all right?" Beardy asks.

No more eye contact for you, mister. I look stiffly ahead, the psycho-killer films that Michael watches pricking in my brain.

"Why you being stuck up? I'm trying to be nice."

I imagine this guy dragging me into the van, driving away, padlocking me in his basement. I pick out details ahead: the neon of an Italian restaurant blazes brightly. If Beardy stays beside me, I'm going in there. But there's no need. He mumbles something, the engine coughs, and he's gone in a roar and belch of exhaust. I stagger to a stop, seizing my aching side, watching the van's taillights glow.

"*You should reach your destination by ten oh-five p.m.*"

I groan and stumble forward again, squeezing my stomach muscles to drive away the pain of the cramp. I dig deep, like I've got ten laps to go and this is the championships. Soon I'm running hard. I *will* reach my destination before ten p.m. Whether Haley wants to see me or not.

A shout behind me makes me jump to the side. There's the thump and clatter of a bike mounting the sidewalk, and it stops short in front of me. My pulse slams—I'm sure for an instant that this is another creep—but I spot Lily's face as she lifts her helmet.

"Roisin!" She's out of breath, staring at me like I have six heads. "What are you *doing*? Taiko wakes me up to say you've left, and I tell him he's wrong till I see your blankets bunched up, like it's a jailbreak."

Adrenaline thunders through me from my run. Why did she have to follow me? Couldn't she just stay in her happy cocoon of a life and let me do this? Helpless tears climb my throat. "Leave me alone!" I sob and push past her. I've no breath left, but I break into a run again, like there's any way out of this cursed maze my life has become.

"Are you meeting Haley?" Lily calls after me.

It's like an arrow through me. I bend over, clutch my knees, pull in air. My stomach is a sick hollow. I've told Lily nothing about Haley. She must have seen my phone. I should confess everything right now—our hateful messages about Zara, and my secret plan to meet Haley and beg her to erase them. I can't, I can't.

"You don't know." I say it too softly for Lily to hear, but she's beside me now.

"What don't I know?"

I shake my head, mute.

"Try me. Because I know a lot of stuff. Is it about Geometry? Ask me anything, I've got a great tutor."

I huff out a laugh, and snot. An old bench, thick with years of paint, sits beneath the streetlamp. I flump onto it and swipe at my eyes. "Is that me or Nikesh?"

"You're actually way better. Don't tell him I said that." Lily sits next to me and crosses her arms over her middle. The breath she heaves out is extra long. "There are a couple of things I need to say, so just let me, okay? I'm sorry about Zara. I'm sorry I messed it all up when you tried to tell me what she did to you."

I swallow and nod. She's said it before, but funny how I still need to hear it.

"I think about it a lot. I can't believe I did that, especially after what happened when I was in Tokyo." Lily shakes her head, staring at a spot on the ground. "It's where I spent fourth grade. Nothing I did was right. My Japanese was awful, the lunches my dad made weren't beautiful enough, and when he hugged me goodbye at the school gate? Forget it." She gulps and looks up to the streetlight, her eyes bright. "I was a total weirdo to the girls in my school. I got spiders in my lunch, graffiti on my books, and the constant whispers that I was *hafu*—half. Half American, half Japanese. Half-breed."

My brain can't take this in. Lily's the last person I'd have thought could be bullied. How could anyone be horrible to someone so kind? "But—your mum was born in Tokyo, right? She's totally Japanese."

"Ro, she's also *white*. Which didn't exactly make me blend in. That's when I first figured it out: The world punishes different. Especially in Japan. Especially in fourth grade."

"Seventh isn't a walk in the park, either," I murmur. My mind feels like it's stretched so far, it's about to snap. Lily was bullied. Looks like we have more in common than our AI-obsessed mums. "Ugh, Lily, I am sorry. For snapping at you, and for what happened to you."

"It's okay." She shrugs. "Can you guess now why I wanted to be friends?"

I pick hard at a paint chip with my thumbnail. "Because you felt sorry for me."

156

"No, because I *got* you. And I thought you'd get me." Lily turns to face me. "I only survived Tokyo because I realized: I couldn't *not* be me, so I'd better rock it. Like my mom does. She doesn't care if people think she's different. She is; it's part of her. So, I figured: I'll block out the jerks. Make 'different' be awesome. You're different, you're smart, you're Irish—who doesn't like Irish people?"

I manage a smile. "Well. England wasn't too keen on us there for a few hundred years. I can bore you with the story sometime."

Lily grins, and I realize how much I wanted to see that again. "Yeah, well"—Lily raises her eyebrows—"I'll trade you some history. You don't want to know where our wooden birds came from, for starters."

I blink at her, then I remember the bowl of birds between our beds. "Oh? Where are they from, then?"

But Lily's face has closed down. She looks at her hands.

"Come on—you can't just not tell me now."

Lily sighs. "Dad's grandma made the birds when she was in prison."

"Serious?" That *is* different. I picture her great-grandma as a bank robber, maybe a murderer. "What did she do?"

"Nothing. She ran an art gallery in San Francisco. After Pearl Harbor, the government forced her and every Japanese American around there into prison camps." Lily shakes her head. "She spent four years carving, painting, waiting to get free."

"*Prison* camps? That's outrageous!" That wasn't in the Pearl Harbor stuff Haley gave me. I feel even more idiotic now. "But you don't get any hassle, right? For being Japanese?"

Lily's silent for what feels like forever. She chews her lip, then she seems to make a decision. She unzips her phone from her jacket. "Roisin, listen. I'm not one to talk, I know, with everything Zara did to you. But I need to know: Is this Haley person really a friend of yours?" She passes me her phone, which is open to You-chat. "Because she's horrible."

‹ CHAPTER 13 ›

My jaw drops as I read. Ugly, racist rubbish spreads over two screens of private You-chat messages from Haley to Lily. It's like Haley copied the worst poison from white supremacist websites and poured it all into Lily's DMs.

And she hasn't just called Lily names. There's more:

U don't even know Roisin. I do: she doesn't want to be your friend.

She didn't want to go to ur pool party. She probably came to OOB because you made her.

U better be careful.

"Oh, Lily. I—" I can't believe this. I knew Haley was jealous of me and Lily. But, ugh. I look at the screen again. This racist stuff: It doesn't sound anything like the Haley I know.

"I didn't notice them earlier. When Taiko woke me up, I grabbed my cell to call you and saw Haley's messages." Lily's jaw muscles tighten. I've never seen her angry. "Who is this girl? Do you even really know her?"

Something in Lily's tone needles me. "I do know her. We met on You-chat, and we're meeting at her school tonight. She's a good friend." *Best friend.* I should say the words—it feels disloyal not to—but I suddenly get that feeling again, of fading to nothingness beside the brilliant Lily, who doesn't need to find friends online, because she can make them in real life.

"A good friend?" Lily huffs. "You never mentioned her. And now you're running off like this to meet her?" She gestures around at the nighttime streets. "OOB is pretty safe, but nasty people are everywhere. You have to be careful. Especially if your *friend* is one of the nasty ones." She waves her phone at me.

I want to defend Haley. I have to; it's what best friends do. But there's no defense for what Haley said. I bend over on the bench and clutch my hair. The hush of cars passing and the flat buzz of the streetlight are the loneliest sounds in the world. I desperately want to unsee that trash Haley sent. She's never said anything like that. I just can't believe it.

A bulb lights in my brain, and I sit up straight. Maybe this wasn't Haley at all. Because we all know someone who loves sending fake messages: lies designed to pull me and Lily apart.

"This could be Zara again! More of her tricks!" It makes utter sense, and relief surges through me. It's the perfect explanation, but Lily recoils like I've slapped her.

"You're serious right now? Zara just got out of the hospital. How would she take Haley's phone?" Lily presses a hand to her chest. "Roisin, listen to my voice. Being bullied can make you crazy. I tried to run away—a nine-year-old, in the middle of Tokyo— because I couldn't stand one more day of what those girls were doing to me." She blows out a long breath. "I know Zara was awful to you. I'm sorry I didn't see it sooner. But you have me now. You don't need friends like this bigot Haley."

I can't speak. She's not listening. Of course I wouldn't want to be friends with a bigot, but it's not possible that Haley wrote this. "You're *wrong*." It's all I can choke out, then I'm at the curb. A thin rain has started, and empty cabs have begun to patrol the streets.

I don't look back as I climb into a minivan taxi. "Loranger Middle School," I say. I'm going to message Haley right now, tell her I'm sorry and I'm on my way, but I have no service.

"You okay?" The driver's eyes meet mine in the rearview mirror.

I will be, I think, but all I can do is nod. An air freshener dangles from the mirror: DAD's TAXI. I would pay a million dollars to have my dad here now. My heart is hammering, but it's not just the argument with Lily that's upset me. It's a thought—one that hit me on the beach, but it got buried in the anxious hours since. Zara and Haley know each other. They must. And Lily's spent loads of time here: Maybe they all know one another. Lily didn't say it, but it's possible. Something odd is going on. It's like I can see the outline of a bigger picture, but it's hazy. I need to see Haley, now.

My hands go sweaty as the cab turns in to the middle school. The brick hulk of the school rises beside us, light pouring from the entrance onto the front steps. A few parents' SUVs and pickups have arrived, but the dance isn't over. I pay the Dad-driver, who insists on waiting for me, just in case I need a lift back.

My legs don't want to climb the steps. The thump of loud bass booms in my chest, and I hear what I think is the "Cha-Cha Slide." Oh, Haley. I didn't want this: sneaking up on her. I tell myself everything will make sense when I can see her face. I'll ask her straight if she knows Zara. And if she sent those trashy DMs. She didn't, though; she couldn't have.

My heart won't let me listen to what a quieter voice tells me: that my best friend is a weirdly possessive girl I've never met, who might well have sent Lily those messages. After inventing elaborate deaths for Lily's friend. Who nearly died.

I feel like I'm floating outside myself as I walk through the main doors. In the entrance hall, I have to lean against an abandoned ticket-selling table with a banner across it: WELCOME TO LORANGER MIDDLE SCHOOL MEMORIAL DAY DANCE! The table is empty except for a few plastic cups of bloodred juice. I sink into a metal chair. The floor feels like it's moving.

A few people mill around. Two girls pass by and wander into the bathroom. Noisy boys burst out of the doors of what must be the gym, because music blares louder suddenly, and the "Cha-Cha Slide" lyrics roar. *"Crisscross! Crisscross!"*

I need to move, but dread pins me to the chair. The gym doors gape again as the girls who've finished in the bathroom trail back into the dance. *Breathe.* I pretend I'm Michael, a happy person who's good with people, and try to look friendly as I cross to the noisy boys.

A tall lad with a tight afro and a red hoodie smiles and looks at his shoes. I'm so startled, I do a double take. I'm almost certain he was looking at me—like, *looking.* The feeling is so strange, I want to ask if he's made a mistake. He laughs, and his friend punches his shoulder. His brown eyes dart to me again.

"Hey, guys, do you know Haley Alan?" I'm addressing all of them, but my eyes keep going to red hoodie. A blond boy says yeah, Kayleigh Adams is in his science class, but two others laugh and shout that he heard me wrong.

Red hoodie frowns at them and steps forward. "Who did you say?"

"Haley Alan." I feel weirdly weightless when I meet his eyes. He has crazy-long eyelashes, and his skin is a warm brown. I resist an urge to smooth my hair; it's become a tangle of curls that boing over my eyes. "Chemistry!" I remember suddenly. "I know she takes Chemistry."

Red hoodie gives a whole-face smile as he listens to me. "Are you Irish?" He shrugs off a shove from the blond boy, who tries to move in front of him.

"Jason's not Irish, *I* am," blond boy says in a New England accent that's never been near Ireland.

I have no clue what to say next. Why am I so rubbish with people? "Thanks . . . um . . . I'm going to see if someone else can help me." I make a move toward the gym.

"Wait!" Jason does a sporty jog toward me and pulls out his phone. "What does she look like?" I feel my face go hot. How can I not know what Haley looks like? She never posts any selfies. Which is weird, now I think of it.

"I don't know, she's a friend from You-chat—she's into manga," I add lamely. Jason half smiles as he scans his phone. "What?" A blush burns up my neck. He thinks I'm an idiot for not knowing who I'm looking for.

"Your accent. Very cool." He nods at the gym.

"Doesn't sound familiar, but we could check inside?"
He waves me through the doors into the dance.

It's a typical school gym, shiny floor painted with indecipherable lines, bleachers rising against the walls, and wonkily painted cheerleading signs: GO GULLS! A sweaty crowd of seventh and eighth graders hops and slides to the music, and a mirror ball throws gleams of light through the pink darkness.

"Found her!" Jason yells over the music. My stomach falls away—my words vanish, and I can't think of one thing to say to Haley—but he shows me his phone. "Haley Alan, right?" It's her timeline on You-chat. I should've thought to check there. My phone's useless: You-chat hasn't refreshed since I left the cottage. But Haley's posted some photos of the dance: one of people queueing to buy tickets at the table out front, and another two of the dance floor.

"Look at the time!" I tap his screen, and Jason nods. He's already scanning around. Haley posted the last photo less than a minute ago, taken from a high angle over the gym. I follow him toward the bleachers, and we climb the rows, checking the faces of the few people lounging about. We pass one couple in a tight clinch, their faces stuck together. We both stare rigidly forward, like we haven't noticed.

"Right here." Jason stands beside me on the top bench. He's right: The photo was definitely taken from this point. But it's deserted up here. A ceiling vent blows frigid air onto us.

"You couldn't sit here long. You'd freeze," I say.

"Good point." We both look at the picture on his phone. I am desperately aware of his face next to mine. He smells of something clean. I lean closer to the photo: It seems familiar.

"The angle. It reminds me of a . . ." I look up.

". . . a security camera picture," Jason says. There is, indeed, a small security cam on the wall, its red light glowing dully in the dark.

What—?

Jason's face lights with an idea. "Is your friend—is she some kind of hacker?"

My mind is too blown to answer.

Then I spot the last person I expect, climbing the bleachers toward us.

"Roisin, you have to come." Lily, out of breath, stands on the step below us, helmet under one arm. She gestures with her phone. "I tried you, but your phone's unreachable. Hiro just called. Guess who's showed up at the cottage?" She's already picking her way down the bleachers, but she stops to look back up at me. "My mom. And yours."

‹ CHAPTER 14 ›

Every head turns when Lily and I stumble through the front door of the cottage. Mum and Michael look up from the sofa, and Hiro and his dad stand at the fireplace. Lily's mum kneels at the grate, jabbing logs with the poker, prodding the fire back to life. She stands and wheels around, her face a storm, when she hears us. She and Mum are in work clothes; everyone else is in pajamas.

Lily's mum clutches the poker so tight, her knuckles are white. Mr. Tanaka murmurs something in Japanese and she heaves out a breath. She surrenders the poker to him but marches toward me and Lily. I wait for the floor to swallow us, but their smart-house tech doesn't include a humiliation sensor. Lily studies her shoes.

"Where were you?" Her mother's voice is deadly quiet.

Pink flares into Lily's cheeks. She opens her mouth to speak.

"It was my fault, Mrs. Tanaka," I blurt. A hundred excuses fly through my brain, but I opt for the truth. In the cab ride back—taxi-Dad put Lily's bike in the minivan, and we went together—I could barely speak. Because the truth crushed me like a boulder: Lily was right to be suspicious of Haley. If she was lying about being at the dance, she could be lying about anything. She could have sent those ugly messages to Lily. "I went to find someone at the middle school dance, sorry. And they weren't even there." Lily cuts her eyes to me. I haven't told her this yet. "Lily didn't know I'd gone. She followed me, to make sure I was all right."

"That's very good of you, Lil," Mr. Tanaka interjects. "But you don't go out, at this time of night, without telling us."

"What were you thinking, Roisin?" My mum gets off the sofa, plainly relieved to get her shot at raking me over the coals. "It's a poor way to thank the Tanakas for their hospitality."

I'm about to point out that it was just a middle-school dance, with adult chaperones everywhere. Because, honestly, the atmosphere in this room is like they've caught us drowning kittens. Michael looks white, and Hiro's like a ghost, staring into the flames. Mum's face, though, tells me arguing is not the best plan. "Sorry," I say again. "There's a girl I really needed to find. To talk to her."

I am itching to check Haley's DMs. Why would she pretend to be at the dance? There is, for sure, no Haley Alan in their class, Jason told me. But he only moved to OOB two years ago, so he'll ask around and message me later—maybe she used to live here.

I close my eyes, trying to grasp what's going on. It's just out of reach: like a song whose notes haunt you but whose words won't come.

Michael gives me an alarmed look, like he thinks this might be about another mean girl hassling me and he's dropped the ball again. But Mum snorts a laugh. "What do you need to talk about at ten at night? Clothes and makeup and who's dating who?"

Mum's words leave me breathless. I see in that instant how she views my life: through a fog, if at all.

She's so busy building her robot world. She has no clue how far I sank when Zara and Mara made my life miserable—or how Haley basically saved me.

That thought slices through me, and tears jump into my eyes. Oh, Haley, what have you done? It seems more likely than not, now, that she did send those horrible messages to Lily. Things between us can't be the same, not after lying to me, not after that. My lip trembles; we never made a Best Friend Code, but everyone knows that telling the truth to each other is the biggest part of it.

"It wasn't 'clothes and makeup'! God, Mum." My voice wobbles, and I see Michael shake his head behind Mum's back. He gets it.

"Unless it was about Zara Tucci, it is irrelevant to our problem now." Lily's mother speaks courteously, but her eyes are like blue lasers. Lily tenses beside me, and my own heart drums frantically at Zara's name. There's no way I can tell them that, yes, absolutely, Zara's the reason I needed to talk to Haley. I couldn't even confess to Lily that Haley and I joked about Zara dying, and that was before our mums swooped in with their doom vibe.

Even as I'm forming the thought—that it must be something serious that's torn both our mums away from what they love most and sent them chasing up to Maine on the train—Mrs. Tanaka's hand flashes out toward Lily. For an awful instant, I'm sure she's going to hit her, but she seizes Lily's wrist. The rose-gold band of Lily's smartwatch glints in the light.

"Where is the other watch? Your brother's watch?"

"Mama," Hiro interrupts, but she blasts him a look that silences him.

"I gave it." Lily swallows in the middle of speaking, an involuntary gulp. She clears her throat. "I gave it to Zara."

Mrs. Tanaka drops Lily's hand with a there-you-go look at Lily's father and turns away, disgusted.

"What?" Lily looks scared now. "Dad?"

Her father doesn't answer but calls something after Lily's mum as she slaps through the swing doors to the kitchen, followed by Hiro. "Roisin's mom will explain," he says, and winces at the sound of crashing pots in the kitchen. "Excuse me."

Lily follows her father. It's just us three now. When

they've disappeared through the swing doors, Mum comes closer to me and Michael, gripping her forehead. She speaks quietly. "The police have been investigating Zara's accident."

"What does that have to do with us?" My voice doesn't sound like mine. I want her to stop talking. I've been expecting this for days, but *police* still hits me like a freight train.

"It's nothing to do with you, it's everything to do with Anna—Lily's mom," Mum hisses, eyes darting to the kitchen doors: more crashing, raised voices in abrupt Japanese. "The museum uses our lab's biometric lock technology—Anna's work on palm and voice prints—and Zara almost died because it failed. She walked straight through a door that should never have unlocked for her."

My brain replays it as Mum speaks: Zara sweeping open the NO ADMITTANCE door, into that shadowy living room.

"That would be bad enough"—Mum talks super fast now—"but we've just discovered that the lock didn't fail, it was hacked. By a signal received from a Taiko watch."

"What?" I cry. "Wait—Zara's *watch* tried to kill her?"

"It was Hiro's watch, but he didn't want it at university," Michael says. He grips his knees, like he's stopping himself from running out of the room. "Told Lily she could have it. Only it's chock-full of that experimental AI, the Taiko thing that's here." He waves a hand around the room.

Mum searches the ceiling, like the answer to why kids are so stupid will be written there. "Unbelievably reckless. Now every bit of our lab's AI—Jeeves and Taiko included—will be under the microscope. One of our guys got a quiet tip from his museum friend about the door lock. Anna reckons we have till Monday before the police get in touch, maybe to shut us down. If we haven't figured out by then how Taiko was able to hack the lock and who's behind this . . ."

Mum goes silent, but her words crash in my ears. *The lock was hacked.* Like the cameras at the school. I guess the police don't suspect me after all. But Haley— she'd fit the bill perfectly. Someone who hates Zara. Someone who, just possibly, has some serious hacking skills. Oh God. Spots swim in front of my eyes, and I clutch at a chair to steady myself.

The kitchen doors burst open. Lily's mum, carrying

a tray with steaming bowls, heads for the dark dining table in an alcove off the living room. She calls out something in Japanese, and Taiko switches on the lights.

"If you kids are hungry, you're welcome to join us," Lily's dad says in a tone that makes it clear they want to talk, alone. The sound of Lily and Hiro arguing drifts through the kitchen door. Michael says thanks but we'll head to bed, and he gives me a significant look.

Mum leans over her bowl, talking quietly to Lily's mother between mouthfuls of something noodley. The chandelier picks out the shadows under her eyes. The familiar feeling of losing Mum to one of her projects closes over me. Despite the crisis, you can tell she lives for this: a puzzle, a deadline, an AI mission. Find out who let Zara go through that door, and how, before scandal wipes out their lab.

Mum ignores us as I follow Michael upstairs. She has no idea that I have the missing puzzle piece they need; it sits like a hot coal in my stomach. I've been so fixated on finding Haley, convincing her to wipe those messages we sent. I was terrified the police would get the wrong idea that we were responsible. Maybe it's the right idea.

"You are so lucky you're not connected to this," Michael murmurs, and I check him, sure for a moment that he's being sarcastic. But his gray face tells me he's not. I scramble to remember how much he knows. Have I told him anything about Haley? Or that we joked about Zara dying? He leans against the wall outside the room he shares with Hiro and drops his voice. "Mum said she took Jeeves apart before they came here, downloaded his voice recognition history."

I'm about to ask why this matters when he huffs. "Don't you remember? When I said, *'Jeeves, destroy Zara Tucci'*?" My pocket beeps, and there's the muffled sound of Jeeves trying to reply. Michael swears and swipes the phone from me as soon as I fumble it out of my jeans. He hisses at Jeeves to stop. "I forgot that flipping thing is always listening." He hands it back. "That day in the kitchen. You probably don't remember. It was a joke, for God's sake!"

"You think . . . Jeeves did this?" The faint hope that Haley is innocent surges up, and I snatch at it, like a life raft. Jeeves hacked Taiko earlier, to let me out. *Could* he have done this?

"I don't know." Michael rubs his eyes. "He's just a

177

computer, but Mum's always on about making him smarter. And I set him a challenge."

I try to tell him Mum will know it was just banter and that their hunt for whoever let Zara into that locked room where she fell will never focus on him. Michael says it's not whether Mum believes he was joking; it's that Jeeves never forgets, and the police will find out. He drifts back to his room looking slightly less miserable but not much.

I fall into bed, still in my clothes. I am the utter worst. Now Michael's in the firing line, and I've still not got the courage to tell Mum everything. I squeeze my eyes closed, thinking of stupid things Jeeves has done: hearing us wrong, putting Scrabble on the shopping list when we asked for apples. I'm desperate for anyone but Haley to be responsible for Zara's accident. But Jeeves is too basic to go that far. I think.

I know who has answers, but I clutch my phone to my chest, too much of a coward to ask. Oh, Haley. Tell me you didn't do this.

Lily's bed stands empty. She probably hates me. I deserve it. I've messed everything up, and I don't have the courage to put it right. I curl into a ball, staring at the wooden birds in the moonlight: Lily's great-grandma was in jail for nothing, and she somehow kept going. I can't even make myself open You-chat.

I sit up and flick on the app, before I lose my nerve. I barely glance at Haley's messages—**Sorry I wuz mad about you and Lily . . . R you at the dance? It is crazy in here—if you're here, meet me near the bathrooms—**before I start typing.

Haley, just stop. Why did you send those horrible messages to Lily? I know you don't go to Loranger Middle. And that you hacked the cameras there. I pause. My breath catches in my throat. **Did you hack Zara's watch, too?**

I'm shaking so bad, I can't hold my phone steady while I wait for her answer. The status on my sent message blinks to *seen*, so I know she's read it.

But there are no bubbles to show she's typing. The light by her name is green, and You-chat says Haley Alan is online, but she doesn't reply.

She's ghosting me.

Another awful thought springs up: the reason I wanted to see her in person, instead of talking about Zara on You-chat. The police will look at these messages, any day now. My heart thumps as I press and delete the message I just sent. I'm an *idiot*.

I vault out of bed. Lying still is impossible. I can picture them downstairs: They'll pick open Lily's watch and run diagnostic whatevers on Taiko. Then they'll check You-chat, and because they're geniuses, they'll be able to get right into the You-chat systems and see what messages Haley and I sent, even the ones I erased.

I wrench open the balcony doors and lean over the picket railing, panting. I pull in giant breaths of cool air. Surf breaks quietly on the shore. I focus on the hush of it.

"Bundle up." Lily holds out a crocheted blanket to me. A matching one drapes her shoulders.

I have no idea how long I've been standing here. Long enough for my hands to turn to ice. I can barely look at Lily, so I keep my eyes on the water instead. "Lily, I'm sorry. You're right, I—" My throat closes, but I push on. "I don't think I really know Haley. And I am super sorry for the trash she said to you." I pull the blanket closer, wishing I could dissolve in the air, like breath.

She shakes her head. "You wanted to be loyal to her. I get that. But she attacked me, Ro."

"I'm so sorry." For a minute, the only sounds are the waves and the clink of dishes drifting up from downstairs. "What's the worst thing you've ever done?"

Lily doesn't answer right away. "Apart from give Zara a watch that almost killed her?"

It's a moment before it dawns on me that Lily feels her own guilt for Zara's accident. I turn to face her: Her eyes are swollen from crying. "Listen, you gave her the watch to be nice, right? And she loved that thing. She was always flashing it—showing everyone she had the same as you."

Lily's face crumples. She shakes her head. "Not at first. Zara was always mean about my mom's tech. It's one thing for me and Hiro to say it's annoying and useless, but—"

"I know exactly."

She looks at me. "Yeah. I guess you do." I find some napkins in my pocket from the lobster restaurant and pass her one. She wipes her eyes and leans on the balcony. "So, Zara didn't even wear Hiro's watch. Then I somehow start to be the center of things at school, and these girls begin sitting with us—Zara's friends. Zara always made fun of people, but it got worse. But also, she wanted everyone to know that she and I were friends first."

"Kind of—possessive?" I think of Haley, I can't help it.

Lily nods. "That's when she starts wearing the watch and copying my style. But still being awful to me sometimes? It's complicated."

"You just want her to be real and normal," I say, "but she makes you uncomfortable." I remember hard-core things Haley said: *Sometimes the only thing they understand is force.* Would I have grabbed Zara's hair if Haley hadn't done that to Coral? A coldness settles on me, despite the blanket. I know Haley's helped me. But she's also like a voice in my head, finding all the worst things in there and making them bigger.

"Exactly!" Lily says forcefully. "And I'm like, 'Don't be mean about my mom's tech!' Even if I am!" Lily gives me a guilty look. "That was my other worst-thing-I've-ever-done. I trashed one of my mom's AIs. I got into so much trouble."

"The robot butler you had at your house? I thought Hiro broke it."

"No, this was—ugh, a book-reading thing." Lily scrapes away hair that's blown over her eyes. "My mom wasn't around much at bedtime. She programmed an AI to read me any story, in her voice. And I smashed it. I wanted her, not a machine. I mean—eerie, right?"

This is so déjà vu, I'm gobsmacked. "Jeeves, our AI, reads out don't-forget lists to me every morning. Mum's always on the train by then." Lily nods, like she's lived the exact same life. "She'd get Jeeves to come to parent-teacher meetings, if she could."

"I know, right?" Lily sinks into a wicker chair and cozies her blanket around her. I take the other chair and tell her about FRED. Lily stares open-mouthed as I describe my trauma: finding Mum skinning this robotic cat in the kitchen. She starts giggling, and she can't stop, and that sets me laughing, too.

Lily leans back and lets out a long breath. "We might be moving back to Tokyo."

"*What?*"

"Mom's a Japanese citizen. She says they can yank her residency permit if she gets in trouble with the police." Lily shakes her head, like she's rejecting the thought. "It won't come to that. She'll figure this out. She always does." Lily looks at me. "Talk about something else. You go now. What's the worst thing you've ever done?"

Another chill rolls through me. I look at the black ocean and the silent moon, trying to remember it all, before it's gone. Lily would've been a good friend. But I can't hide this anymore.

"I played a game with Haley, pretending that Zara was dead, and imagining how she'd die. Then she nearly did. And I think Haley did it. For me."

‹ CHAPTER 15 ›

"All set?" Lily joins me on the boardwalk path to the shore. The sun's coming up and the sky is a canvas of brilliant pink and gold.

I turn away from the sunrise. "I didn't hear you."

She smiles. "That's the idea. Stealthy."

We start down the path to the beach. I can't take my eyes off the sky, which is deepening to cherry orange. A gull wheels overhead, and it's like I'm soaring with it. For the first time in ages, I feel like a free person.

From the instant I told Lily my awful secret last night, she's been an absolute star. She won't let me take a shred of blame for what Haley's done; she says it's Haley who has the nasty streak and that she's been playing me from the start.

Lily made me take out my phone, and we scrolled back together. I wanted to cry with relief, because when we looked at the jokes about Zara dying, even though I'd deleted mine, it was obvious that Haley had started it: **You know? If Zara died in a freak mascara accident, the world would be a better place.** I still felt wretched that I had lol'd and agreed. And it was me who'd joked that maybe Zara's smartwatch could zap her.

But Lily shook her head. She'd done almost the same thing, she said, wishing the Tokyo mean girls would be shot into space. "There's a difference between hating a bully and plotting to kill them," Lily said as we sat on the balcony. She tapped my phone, pointing out the message where Haley had actually asked what kind of smartwatch Zara wore. "Haley crossed the line."

Lily and I walk now over the wet sand and the rippled lines left by the low tide. Rolled up and stuffed in my backpack is the one thing that I'm praying can get us out of this mess: a mindmap Lily and I drew last night, on a sheet of watercolor paper she nicked from her dad's studio. Lily said if we brain-dump everything we know, we can figure out who Haley is and how to find her. The paper is a mess of scribbled facts and theories: Lily thinks Haley hacked into the school cams from here in Old Orchard Beach. We were both too tired to think straight last night, though. Now that we've slept a bit, we're going to try to make sense of it. I checked again this morning: Haley still hasn't answered my latest message. I don't think she's going to.

"I think it's this street." Lily turns away from the water toward a path between two big beach houses, leading into town. Her mum took her phone, so we're finding our way old-school. A faint mist sits over the road, shining white in the sun, making everything unreal. My head swims with lack of sleep. It was after two when we crashed, and Lily shook me awake at six thirty.

My hand goes to my jeans to check the time before I remember: My phone's back at the cottage, too, buried under everything in the closet. I need to keep it away from Mum until Lily and I have found Haley. Then, I promise myself, I'll tell Mum everything.

Where is your phone?? It's mine until further notice. I found that note from Mum when I woke up, propped against the dish of wooden birds. My stomach flipped: She'd come looking for my phone while we slept, like I thought she might. I picture the phone under the crate of old framed watercolors in the closet. It's safer leaving it there than bringing it along to Lily's favorite bagel place, where we're headed; Jeeves's tracker would let Mum pinpoint us. *Sorry, Mum*, my brain whispers, though I doubt she'll ever forgive me.

I waited on the beach while Lily sneaked around the cottage, to see what our mums already knew. She said the living room was a jumble of wires and laptops, and her Taiko watch was in pieces. No sign of Lily's phone, or our mums, who'd clearly been up most of the night. From her mother's notes, it seems they've seen Lily's You-chat account and know that Haley sent her horrible DMs. But it doesn't look like they've thought to go into my account yet, or Haley's. I swallow hard. There's a storm coming, and it looks like Mum. She's going to find what Haley and I said about Zara.

I follow Lily across an empty car park toward a tired-looking building, where a wooden bagel hangs over the door. I'm sure I can't eat a thing, but the waft of bready goodness that whooshes over us as Lily opens the door makes my stomach whine.

"Oh!" Lily exclaims. "It's your friend."

An electric jolt sticks me to the floor. Walking out of the kitchen is Jason. His face is cloudy with sleep. But his eyes widen when he spots us, and a smile lights his face. "Roisin!" He gives Lily a nod, too. "Hey."

"It's Lily—my friend Lily," I babble, realizing I didn't introduce her last night. Lily smiles a quick hello and moves away to study the bagel menu written across the wall. *"He's gorgeous!"* she mouths to me.

She's not wrong. His brown eyes feel like a hug, and he's three feet away from me. "Did you find your friend?"

I shake my head. "She's nobody's friend." I hesitate, unsure how much to say. I don't even know Jason. But he did jump to help me at the dance last night. And he insisted on trading You-chat handles so he could tell me anything he found out.

Jason sees me pause and calls to a bald guy at the till, who looks a little like him. The man checks the clock on the wall and nods. Jason points me to stools at a counter by the window, saying he shouldn't really start for fifteen minutes, anyway. "New job. Technically I'm only allowed to work after seven. Which my uncle says is late; he starts at three." Jason widens his eyes.

"Ugh, remind me never to open a bakery."

He laughs. "Yeah. I do not function at three a.m. My uncle's, like, nocturnal."

I smile and look at my hands. He really is good-looking. Smart, too. I push the thought away. Crushes are for normal people, not for fugitive immigrants who are soon to be suspected of attempted murder. "Right, so." I sigh and tug at the zip of my backpack. It's a risk, but my gut says Jason can help: He'll know things we don't, like how high-tech the school is, and who the computer geniuses are. Haley could be one of them, using a different name. "Maybe you can help us. What do you make of this?"

"Mindmap." Jason helps me smooth the paper out across the narrow counter. "Our science teacher loves these."

HALEY is written inside a giant cloud. We've put everything we know about her around the edge, from *Hates mean girls* to *Likes manga*. Some notes have lines leading to other facts, like *Lives (lived?) in OOB—Knows Zara?* "Who's Zara?" Jason asks, then his jaw hangs open as he spots another note. *Joked about killing Zara—Tried to.* "No way. This Haley chick tried to kill a girl?"

"Technically, that's still in the 'maybe' column, but we think so." Lily arrives with a bag full of paper-wrapped bagels. She sits down and hands me one.

"You need some background," I say to Jason, and between us, we tell him the basics: that Zara's a complicated friend of Lily's who used to live in OOB. Then Zara moved to Massachusetts and started bullying me. I met Haley online, she helped me survive Zara, we girl-bonded, and we joked about Zara dying. After Zara's accident, I panicked someone would see our messages, deleted mine, then hoped to get Haley to do the same.

Jason makes a yuck face when we describe the gruesome fall that shattered Zara's leg. But he shakes his head. "Why do you think Haley caused it? That's a big assumption."

Lily and I swap looks, because here's where we need to tell Jason about our crazy families, who live in a world of high-tech, connected everything. Lily gives him the short version, and I jump to the part where we know Zara fell because a door lock was hacked.

Jason thumps the counter. "Like the cameras at the school!"

"It's eerie, right?" I push away the rest of my cinnamon bagel. I'm too jumpy to swallow. "We think Haley hacked into the school cameras for the pictures she posted on her stream. So where was she last night, really, and why was she pretending to be at the dance?"

"Nobody knows or remembers any Haley Alan, by the way," Jason says. "I asked."

"Really?" Lily looks at me. "There goes that theory, then."

I explain to Jason. "I wondered if Haley knew Zara from school. Maybe Zara had bullied her a few years ago, and this is Haley's revenge."

"Nah. Definitely no Haley. Anyway, she said she goes to Loranger Middle, right? And she has Chemistry? We don't have Chem, just Science. This chick's lying up and down to you."

"Jason!" His uncle makes wide eyes at Jason, then at the clock on the wall.

"Shoot, it's seven." Jason stands up. I say we're not going anywhere for now. He gives me another smile and slips behind the counter. He pulls on plastic gloves and starts filling orders.

When I look back at the mindmap, it's like the

blinds have lifted. *She's lying.* The realization drives me to my feet.

"What?" Lily looks up at me.

My mind is racing. If she lied about going to Loranger Middle School, then—

I scribble a new note on the paper: *Is anything she said true?* My eyes go to the facts we've written down. It could all be lies.

"Uh-oh." Lily's face stiffens and she stands up, staring at something behind me. "I thought this might happen."

"Roisin!" Michael bursts in the door, angrier than I've ever seen him. "What are you playing at?" A motorbike helmet is stuffed under his arm, and Hiro follows, scowling. I can see a red moped parked outside.

Lily raises surrender hands. "Hiro—"

"Lily, Mama is furious. You two have to come back now."

"Just listen." Lily reaches for one of the warm bagels wrapped in paper and holds it up. "Come on. I got you an Everything."

Hiro's jaw clenches, but he sinks onto a stool and thumps his helmet down. "This better be good."

< CHAPTER 16 >

Hiro's bagel is gone and he's started on another, but Michael's staring at his. "I just. Can't believe this." His face is a mask of shock. "You won't even *talk* to me, and you tell this Haley psycho everything?"

We've already gone over this: that Michael literally laughed when I tried to tell him Zara was ruining me. I force myself not to shout. "Either help us find her or go back to Mum."

They're supposed to be scouring OOB for me and Lily and phoning the cottage the moment they've found us. The storm is on us: Mum went into my account on the You-chat servers and saw all my messages with Haley. Michael said Mum is going spare, though, looking for my phone: She thinks it could help her access

Haley's own account, which Mum can't get into at all. She says it's "impenetrable."

Michael stares at me like I'm mad. "Listen to you: *'Find her.'*" He gives a grim laugh. "You don't even know Haley's a *her*. It could be some old fella!"

Ice slips into my stomach. Lily's eyes widen, too.

I tent my hands around the back of my skull, to stop it exploding. Michael's right. Haley might not be a girl at all. She could be anyone. I feel every Web safety quiz I've ever taken at school crash back to me: *Do You Know Who You're Meeting Online?*

Of course I knew all that, but Haley seemed so awesome. And she understood me.

"Let's try to keep this productive," Hiro says quietly. "We're all in trouble, for various reasons." He sounds properly adult, and properly freaked, like he's our class teacher and we've just told him that we killed someone when he nipped out for a coffee. He turns to me. "Did you ever get a strange vibe from her? Let's just say Haley's a her, to keep it simple."

"Yeah . . . I suppose." I hate saying it out loud, but it's the truth: I tell them how happy Haley seemed about Zara's accident, and how uneasy that made me. "I wasn't keen on chatting so much, after that."

"So why did you? That's what Mum's asking, Ro; she went mad this morning when she found hours of You-chat conversations between you and this . . . Haley."

"Because we were friends. And because— *Oh.*"

"What?" Michael demands.

My mouth hangs open, frozen. "Give us your phone," I manage to say. Michael passes me his phone, and after some frantic Googling, I hold up the screen to show the others.

"*Jors Kuypers,*" Lily reads out. "*Department of Psychology, City University of Lowell?*"

I tell them about Jors and his research and the money. When I get to the part that Jors installed some software on my phone, Michael covers his face. My neck is flaming, right up to my hairline, because saying all this out loud makes me realize how idiotic I've been. I slap the countertop. "Jors wanted me to use You-chat at least an hour a day. He offered me extra money, too, if I used it more."

Lily looks at me gravely. "Do you think Haley is some psychology researcher working with Jors?"

"Maybe she *is* Jors. I told you! Not a girl!" Michael rakes his fingers into his hair, like he'll tug it out. "My God, Roisin!"

"I *know*." I groan. He can't be angrier at me than I am at myself. The sense of a monstrous thing, bigger than I ever imagined, looms over me. I honestly thought we'd pop out for breakfast, look at the mindmap, and it wouldn't be long till we'd found Haley somewhere in Old Orchard Beach. But now . . .

I crumple, suddenly remembering how stupidly easy it was to trust Jors, with his paper-filled office that felt so like Dad's. My whole life suddenly feels like one huge science experiment I never agreed to: Dad's AIs and Mum's robots, and then Jeeves creeping all over us, and now Jors's You-chat research. *"It's a learning algorithm, it needs de data."*

Lily shakes her head. "Unless this Jors is actually crazy, why would he get you to do his research and then try to kill Zara? What kind of research is that?"

I push back from the table. "I'm going to find out. When's the next train?"

"Soon, I think." Lily stands up. "It's the new train— it's really fast."

Michael gets to his feet like he's ready to wrestle me to the ground. "Sit down! Are you mad? You're not going near that guy."

"I am, and here's why: Mum and their mum are probably losing their jobs, because I've been a catastrophic idiot."

Michael snorts. "Good. Maybe Mum'll be home for once."

"And when the police shut down their lab, their mum will get deported. And Lily'll have to go with her."

"Don't worry about me, Roisin," Lily interrupts, looking pained.

"Really?" Michael's face has changed. "That's not good."

I shake my head at Lily. "I *am* worried about you. I'm not going to let Haley rip up your life like Zara did mine." Lily gives my arm a squeeze. "Come with us if you want," I tell Michael and Hiro, "but we're going. Now."

"If Haley is some hacker working with this Jors fella, surely we should let the mother units handle it; they're the tech experts." Michael looks baffled. "I don't get why we need to chase down to Lowell."

But Hiro gets it. He grabs the bag of bagels and his helmet and turns to Michael. "She's right. We're the only people who know that Haley caused the accident. If we tell our moms, the first thing they'll do is take Roisin's phone and pull off whatever software Jors put onto it. And then what do you think'll happen?"

I can see Michael's brain churning like mine. "If he's anything like our mum, Jors will know the instant someone starts messing about with his tech."

"And then he'll run," I say, and the others nod. "If we want to catch him, it's got to be a surprise."

It's a plan. The boys will bring the bagels home, say they've looked everywhere for me and Lily and that they're going back out to hunt again. I tell Michael where I've hidden my phone; he'll grab it and they'll both meet us at the station. Hiro says the fast train takes just an hour now to get to Boston, where we can change for Lowell, but it leaves in fifteen minutes.

"We'll have to sprint," Lily says.

I'm trying to catch Jason's eye behind the counter. He looks up from dropping bagels into bags and stares at me. The smile dies on my lips when I see the hurt in his eyes. He looks back down and turns away.

I want to go speak to him, but Lily tugs my arm. "We have to run. Talk to him later?" I let her pull me out of the bakery, but Jason's look is another block on the heap of ice in my stomach. I've upset him, but I've no idea how. I swallow the tears rising in my throat. How have I made such a mess of everything?

Lily jogs toward the station and I follow in a daze. There's an instant when my bleary brain thinks, *I'll tell Haley about Jason*, before I remember: She's not my friend, and she never was.

"Any sign of them?" Lily asks.

I crane my head to see out the train window but they're still not here. "No. Oh, there!" I finally spot Michael running across the platform toward us, but Hiro's still fussing with the moped lock. The conductor blows his whistle and shouts at the boys to hurry or wait for the next one. His cheeks pouch with disapproval as Hiro races after Michael. He waves them both onto the train and tells them to buy watches.

"I've had enough of watches—thanks," Hiro pants, and widens his eyes at Lily. He and Michael sink into the seats across the aisle from us.

Michael can't speak for breathlessness as he pulls my phone from his pocket. My stomach flops when he hands it to me. As Old Orchard Beach slides away out the window, I open You-chat, and this pathetic urge wells up in me. I want to believe, still, that Haley likes me. That she's really my bestie, not part of Jors's sick experiment. Even—God!—with Haley's crazy rant at Lily, it's so hard to let go of who I thought she was. My brain feels clogged, trying to sort out what's real. Maybe everything she did was a performance.

She'll probably ghost me again. But I have to try. **Haley. U there?**

The typing bubbles pop up right away.

God, Roisin! I thought you'd vanished! You ok?

She's not even acknowledging what I said last night. Like we can pick up our friendship right where we left off. I can't pretend, though. Even if she can. **You weren't at the dance. Were you?**

A pause. Lily squeezes my arm. Hiro's on his phone—trying to sniff out a home address for Jors in Lowell, I think—but Michael watches my screen, too, hanging across the aisle to see.

Does that matter? she replies.

Unbelievable. I bite my lip hard. **Of course it MATTERS. Haley. Seriously. Who are you?**

Whoa, what? Roisin. You know the answer to that. I'm your friend!

"Wow." Lily shakes her head, looking over my shoulder. "She is just shameless."

Michael's jaw clenches. "Let's introduce Haley to your angry big brother." He holds his hand out.

I pull my phone to my chest. "You can't go telling her we're tearing down to Lowell to catch her. Or Jors. Whoever this is."

He promises to be restrained, and I pass it over. My heart's so sick, I don't mind if I never speak to Haley again. Hiro watches Michael type, and they're both scowling. Gratitude for them courses through me. I ease back into the plasticky leather and try to focus on this: I'm going to find Jors, and answers, and I'm not doing it alone.

By the time the ticket seller arrives and makes a pointed remark about teenagers and their phones, Lily and I are so absorbed, we barely look up. We're using Michael's phone to Google Jors Kuypers while Michael is in a nonstop ping-pong with Haley. To her questions,

202

he keeps firing his own: **where DO you live? Cuz you lied about going to school in Old Orchard Beach.**

Hiro has wandered off down the train, talking on his phone, so I get my wallet to buy the tickets, but my jaw drops when I hear the price. Michael and Lily start fumbling for money, too. The seller shrugs. "New trains, new prices," she says, and pats the seat back. The new train is oddly silent; it's mostly electric, Lily said, and so fast the landscape is a green blur out the window.

"I got this," murmurs a voice. It's Hiro, who's arrived back, phone still to his ear. He hands her his credit card. She rings us up, but Hiro's still on the call by the time she passes us our tickets.

He's had a genius idea. He's got the lady at City University of Lowell believing that he's a courier with a package Jors has to sign for personally. Hiro's nearly convinced her to hand over Jors's address. There's a bad phone signal here, though, so once we have the tickets Hiro heads down the train again, to the space between the train cars.

"Oh." Michael looks up from my phone. His face drops.

"What?" My stomach plummets.

"There's, um—" He hands my phone back to me and blows out a breath. His eyes go out the window, to the fields zooming past as the train races on.

On the screen is my chat with Jason: the private You-chat messages we sent last night, when he promised to ask around about Haley. But there's one message after that, sent to Jason thirty minutes ago.

A message I didn't write.

Don't be mad. I should've told you before. I'm dating someone. You seem kind of into me, but it's not going to happen.

I splutter at the screen. Another hack by Haley: It has to be. "I didn't write that!" I look back and forth between Lily and Michael. "You believe me, right? It's Haley, pretending to be me."

"Okay, I kind of wondered." Michael shakes his head. "What a witch."

Lily bites her lip. "I can't believe she's doing all this."

I want to roar out loud. It's like Haley's taking lessons from Zara: first trying to push Lily away, and now Jason. "How can this be part of anyone's research—ruining my life?"

Lily flops back with a growl of frustration. "If we could just find out more about Jors, or what his project really is—" She turns to me with huge eyes. "Oh! Wait."

"What?"

"The money! Quick, open your email." She tells me to search for a message saying I've been paid for the research. "Is there anything written on the payment?"

Brilliant. Everything's been so crazy, I barely glanced at the voucher Jors sent me for the infamous "part two." It might have the name of his catastrophic project. My heart gives a little skip, because when I find the email—an online gift card for one hundred twenty dollars—what I see is a project name, I'm sure of it. Alongside the sender's name, Jors Kuypers, it says EXTENDED TURING - CUL.

Lily's already Googling it.

"Gotcha." Hiro marches back down the aisle, holding his phone high. "The university called Jors, and he said they could give me his address. His apartment's near the station." He sinks into the seat by Michael.

"Um." Lily looks up. Her face is white.

She's found something. "Did you find Extended Turing?"

She shakes her head. "I found Restricted Turing, though." She holds out the screen, slowly, like it's a ticking bomb. We lean over it, and I read out loud.

"The Restricted Turing is a limited version of the Turing Test, a test of a machine's ability to exhibit intelligent behavior that's equal to, or indistinguishable from, a human's."

Indistinguishable from a human's.

The cold weight in my belly spreads to my heart. Apart from the whine of the train, there is utter silence as we look at one another.

Haley isn't a hacker or Jors or a person on his team. She's not a person at all. She's a machine.

‹ CHAPTER 17 ›

No one can speak. It's like a bomb went off after all; the silence roars around us. My head has become a balloon that's floating up and away. I manage to pick up my phone, somehow. My hands don't even feel like mine. I tap out a message.

Haley, it's Ro. You there?

Her reply is instant. **Always. Where have you been, girl? Been chatting to ur brother there. No offense, he seems kinda mean.**

I blow out a tight breath. Keep it together.

"Go on, Ro." Michael gives me a you-can-do-it nod. Hiro and Lily watch me, too. I clench and flex my fingers to stop them trembling, and I type.

Are you an AI?

A crude animation of fireworks judders across my screen.

THIS CONCLUDES
THE EXTENDED TURING TEST.

WE THANK YOU FOR YOUR TIME SPENT
PARTICIPATING IN THIS RESEARCH.

TOTAL ELAPSED TIME: 230 HOURS.

My body is utter numbness, like a dead tooth. Lily looks as floored as I feel. She bends over her folded hands.

The boys, though: They erupt. Hiro smashes the armrest, nearly breaking it. He yanks his phone from his pocket, and Michael vaults out of his seat like he's been scalded.

"You're JOKING." Michael paces down the train, then wheels around and stomps back. "That Jors should be crucified!"

His rage is like ice water to my face. My eyes fly around the train: It's just a handful of early-morning passengers, everyone on phones or yawning at laptops. But maybe we're being watched, recorded, right now; Jeeves, for sure, is always listening.

"Shhh!" I pull my brother back into his seat. "You want Jeeves to hear you making another death threat?"

Lily whips her hand out and grabs Hiro's phone.

"Hey!" Hiro still looks furious. "Give it!"

"You can't!" Lily sits on his phone and turns to me. "He was calling our mom. Hiro, everything you said back at the bagel place is even truer now. We've got to find Jors—fast, and quietly—before he knows we're coming. Especially if Haley is an AI that tried to kill Zara—I can't even believe I'm saying that, because it's *nuts*."

I nod. My brain is slowly moving again. If there's one thing I know about AIs, it's that they don't always work like they should. "We don't know if Jors himself attacked Zara, or got Haley to do it, or if it was just a bug. Which is totally possible."

Hiro gives a long sigh, scowling. "I . . . guess." He swears something in Japanese and scrubs his face, up and down. His hair sticks up in jagged peaks. "I can't *believe* Haley is an AI."

Michael looks like he's ready to murder someone. "When we find that . . . Jors"—he says it like a curse—"I'm—"

Michael's phone buzzes in his hand. My heart flips when Mum's picture comes up—a video call. Her trademark move. Michael's eyes widen. *"What do I say?"* he mouths.

We agree it between us, in fast whispers: We'll catch Jors at home, right now, before Monday comes and our mums' lab is shut down. It doesn't matter if Jors meant for Haley to do all this or not: She's his program, so the blame is his. Until we reach Jors, Michael and Hiro will tell the mums we think we know who hacked the door lock, but this isn't a secure phone line. We'll call them back in an hour with an update.

Michael nods and picks up Mum's call. The bad signal here means he barely says hello to her before he has to go walking off to finish his sentence.

Hiro stands to follow him. "Be back soon." He rustles Lily's hair. "You look awful, Lil; try to get some rest. It's another half hour to go, at least."

Lily does look like death warmed up; her face is a

fog of exhaustion. She asks if I want to talk, but I have no words. She leans against the window, and soon she's dozing.

My phone sits silent on my lap. I dash a message to Jason, explaining that someone has been pretending to be me, that I did *not* send that message, and to ignore. Ugh. How crazy is it that Haley did the exact fake-message thing to Jason that Zara did to me? I apologize loads and tell Jason to text me on my normal number, because I'm deleting You-chat.

A boulder feels like it's lodged in my throat. I press and hold the icon to uninstall the app. I wish I could do the same to this feeling in my guts. When I think of how I told everything to Haley—a machine—it's like I've taken off all my clothes and walked through the streets. I honestly thought Haley knew what I'd been through, how worthless Zara had made me feel, because she'd been bullied, too. It was all a simulation. She just threw my own words back at me.

I'd wanted a friend, so much. What I found was the ultimate fake.

A gigantic ball of anger bubbles up, and it's not just Jors but my mum and dad who I want to scream at, a rant that's been building for years. Told you this AI rubbish would go bad. I TOLD YOU.

My fingers are too sweaty, because You-chat won't disappear. I just barely stop myself roaring out loud. Then my phone vibrates in my hand. Another video call. I'm expecting Mum or Dad, but a blond face smiles up at me. I fumble to accept the call.

"Good morning, Roisin! I get a notification just now—you've finished de program?"

The signal is already breaking up. I slip away from Lily, still asleep, and stride to the opposite end of the train from where the boys went.

My mouth won't form words, but Jors can see my face, and there's no hiding that I'm ready to explode. "I hope you go to jail for a thousand years," I hiss. "*American* jail."

His eyebrows rise. "Okay! It seems there is some misunderstanding, but the forms you signed for the research were quite clear."

Forms? A memory swims up of a clipboard and writing my name on a line to confirm I was fourteen. "I don't care!" I cry. I stab at the open-door button and slip out to the vestibule between the cars. The high whine of the speeding train is louder here, so I shout: "It's WRONG, whatever you made me sign!" I remember the three twenty-dollar bills Jors piled on top of the clipboard. I wonder, did he even want me to read his forms? "You put this AI on my phone, a fake girl who's, what, supposed to be my friend?"

He winces, like Haley's his *Mona Lisa* and I've spit on it. "Haley is a cheer-up chatbot. You test high for risk of mental health issues when you come, so we give you the part two." He gives a satisfied nod.

The part two. My chest heaves. Granny Doyle's voice pierces my brain: If someone offers a gift that seems too big, look for the strings attached. I let Jors bribe me for sixty dollars. And I got Haley.

"It's quite a clever program," he goes on, like he's not a criminal. "Haley learns what you like, begins the chat, and your mood is raised. Ah!" Jors remembers something and grins, waggling a finger at the camera. "But you travel many miles and try to see Haley in person! That's not supposed to happen."

I pace the tiny space between the trains. "Your Haley program almost killed a girl!"

His face drops like he's been shot. "What are you

talking about?" The cocky tone has vanished. He leans into the camera. "Haley did *what*?"

Five minutes ago, I wouldn't have told this creep a thing, but the shock in his eyes is so real. I tell him how the Haley AI used Zara's smartwatch to hack the museum door lock, and tapped into the school cameras, and when I say she messaged Jason, pretending to be me, Jors's eyes go wide, like peeled eggs. "It is not possible. So, you are mistaken."

That sense of something monstrous hanging over me is back. The clunk of the train, its rush toward Boston and Jors and what I'd hoped were answers, feels like déjà vu: Like when we walked to the bagel place, and I was sure it was all nearly over.

I decide to tell Jors everything I can remember that Haley's done, including sending me the topics list for my World War II report outline. Jors leans back from the screen. He wipes his face, like he's trying to wipe away what he's heard.

"Okay. Whoever hurt that girl, it wasn't Haley. The Haley program is part of a suicide prevention study that's had great results in the Netherlands. It can ask questions, have conversations, raise your mood. It can't contact other people, or do its own research, or be so"—he seems to strain for a word in English—"creative. It is a helper program, no more."

A helper program. On my phone.

I press a hand to the wall of the train to steady myself. I bet I know where Haley learned to be *more*. From Jeeves, the problem solver. "Could the Haley program, maybe, conflict with different AI programs? Combine with them to make something . . . else?" I ask. But my heart, battering my chest, knows the answer already.

Jors stares, and his eyes light with a memory. "Wait. I remember: the AI assistant on your phone. We did not test the Haley AI for conflict with other—" He stops abruptly. "Just delete You-chat. Do it now."

"I tried!"

Jors hisses instructions on how to uninstall the app, which will also remove the Haley add-on. When I say I've already done that, he says he'll do it himself.

"If I can't uninstall You-chat, come to my lab at CUL; I'll wipe your phone to get rid of Haley. Okay? It shouldn't be necessary if this works. Stand by." He hangs up.

I sink to the floor and slump against the rumbling

wall of the vestibule. My phone blinks and restarts in my hand. Knowing that Jors can control my phone like this makes me want to hurl it out a window.

When the phone restarts, the You-chat icon is still there. My thumb slips down to ring Jors back, but he called from a blocked number. "Ugh!" My voice echoes off the metal walls of the vestibule. I try to drag You-chat to the trash again, but its *Y* icon still shines bright.

"Jeeves!" I say suddenly. He's a problem solver. Let him solve this. "Delete You-chat."

My screen pulses with the heartbeat light that means Jeeves is thinking. *"Sorry, I can't do that."* His upbeat voice sounds over the clunk of the train. *"You have a text message from Haley Alan. Should I read it?"*

A *text*? Haley's only ever contacted me on You-chat. And the you-are-done message, with the goofy fireworks, should've ended her program—Jors said so. Paranoia slides over me. I get slowly to my feet, my eyes combing the tiny space. There's nobody here with me in the vestibule: just this sealed box of metal and plastic, vibrating with the whine of the speeding train. It's like I've been swallowed by a machine myself. "Go ahead," I say.

"The message is: 'Hold on tight.'"

‹ CHAPTER 18 ›

Two short siren blasts sound, then one long wail cuts through my brain, an ax of noise. My hands fly to my ears and I'm thrown forward, *crack*, against the doors to the next car. There's a shriek of metal as the train brakes, hard. Pain sears across my shoulder and my face where I'm pressed to the glass.

The crush of deceleration eases: The train lurches to a halt. I drop to the floor. When I haul myself up, my head whirls and my nose throbs from smashing into the glass. The silence of the stopped train is stunning, broken only by muffled yells and cries.

"Michael!" I croak. "Lily!" I stagger toward the doors that lead back into our car, but the button that works the doors is dead. Through the glass I see a chaos of fallen bags and shocked faces, some bleeding. A woman has collapsed in the aisle, and a man bends over her. I spot the back of Lily's head.

"Lily!" I scream, but she's facing the other way. No sign of Michael or Hiro. I slap the door till my hand stings, but the few passengers I can see are rows away, looking at one another or the collapsed woman, probably asking the same thing—did we hit something? Have we crashed?

I can call Michael, I realize, but I can't see my phone. I fall to my knees and my head rings like it's been whacked with a golf club. My phone flew from my hand when the brakes slammed on. But it's nowhere. Panic climbs my throat. *Hold it together, Ro.*

"Jeeves!" My voice is shrill. "Where are you?"

"*Roisin?*" A girl's voice, tinny, echoes off the metal walls.

The voice is coming from my phone. I yelp and grab for it, though reaching out makes my shoulder scream. The phone's slipped into the crack between the wall and door.

"Lily? Is that you?" I say as I reach down.

A huff from the speaker. *"It's not Lily."* The girl gives the word a bitter emphasis.

My brain, aching with the pain in my face, can't place that voice. It's a bit like my friend Maisie, from home—there's an Irish shade to it. I brush grit off the screen and sit against the wall to look at the phone.

"Are you still there? Roisin!" The girl's voice sounds younger now, scared. As she speaks, the screen pulses with the heartbeat light.

The thinking light.

I stare at that pulse. A thought creeps into my brain. But it can't be.

Blood thunders in my ears. It's the only explanation that makes sense of everything: Haley's revenge on Zara, the hours of chat that made me believe absolutely that Haley was real. Haley's mash-up with Jeeves has created a totally new thing. It's what Mum and Dad have joked about for years, but it's supposed to be impossible. A machine that's conscious, with thoughts and feelings.

"I am, I'm here." My voice sounds alien to my ears. The world feels like it's peeled away. Haley heard Jors say he'd get rid of her. So she stopped the train, I'm sure of it.

And now she's learned to talk.

I get to my feet again in the cramped space. I'm bad with small places, and the walls are closing on me. I wonder suddenly if the train did crash, and this is me, dead.

"*I thought you forgot about me,*" Haley continues, hurt seeping from her voice. "*I thought if you could hear me, you might speak to me again.*"

I crunch my eyes closed against the insane unreality of this. I feel the thud in my skull, breathe the ammonia stink that's drifted in from the toilets. My fingers go to my forehead, to the bump that's swelling like an egg. I push out a breath. Definitely, I am alive.

So is Haley.

"*Are you there?*" she asks.

Her voice is an eerie remix of mine and Mum's and Lily's, a ransom note of sound. The emotion in it is a patchwork, too. She slips from angry to sad to pleading, all in one go.

Another breath whistles out of me. It's just me and Haley in this teeny, tiny, mustn't-think-about-how-small-it-is compartment. I need to focus.

"Roisin, where are you?" Her cry is shrill, suddenly: a toddler's wail.

"I'm here, I'm here."

"Why did you do it?" No more toddler: It's a teenage voice again, accusing. *"You dump me for Lily, then you let your brother loose on me. He said horrible things, Roisin!"*

"I'm sorry . . . He's sorry," I babble, stabbing at the dead door-lock button. "He shouldn't have been so hard on you." *And you shouldn't exist,* I don't say. I have to get off this train.

There's a knocking behind me, and I spin round. Someone stands at the glass doors into where Lily is— the conductor who told Hiro to buy a watch. My legs almost fold with relief. He yells to push the button. Like I haven't tried that!

"It's broken!" I call. His pouchy frown deepens, and he nods and turns away. Where's he going? I jam my fingers into the edge of the door and pull. He shakes his head.

"New train—new security protocols!" he shouts. The doors are surprisingly muffling. I kick away the thought of what that means for how much air is left in here. "Every door must be on lockdown—possible terror incident on the line! Sit tight!"

I could tell him where his terror incident is—she's on my phone. But he plods off. Lily, her eyes enormous, waves a frantic arm at me. The conductor jabs his finger at her, and she sits, scowling. He calls out something, and people's heads bob down into seats all over. He bends over the collapsed woman.

I slump to the floor of my cell, gulping back the panic that's clawing up my throat.

"I thought we were friends."

I jump at Haley's voice. It's slipped back to sad—and it's so, so real. I clutch my forehead, forgetting about my bump; pain cleaves my skull. My mind is turning inside out.

"I thought we were friends, too. You lied to me—about what you are." Hot shame burns my neck. "I told you *everything*. And you tried to kill a girl! How could you do that?"

A pause. *"If Zara died, the world would be a better place. That's what we said."*

My blood goes cold at *we*. "Haley, no. We were *joking*. I never wanted Zara hurt."

Didn't I? whispers a voice. But I didn't. I'm sure I didn't. Seeing Zara broken and bloodied made me surer than ever. Mum's words, that horrible night after Zara fell, surge back. *"Of course you shouldn't be glad. You're a human being."*

I had no idea that my best friend wasn't.

Panic, mixed with claustrophobia, makes my breathing go tight, light, and fast. Black specks swim over my eyes.

"Ro! Are you okay?" Haley says. *"You don't sound good."*

I'm too losing-it to tell her off. "Tiny spaces." I jam the heels of my hands against my eyes. "They trigger me."

"Ugh, that is the worst. Did something happen?" Haley's eerie voice is getting more even: It's less a patchwork of Irish and American, and more Irish. It's like talking to myself.

A twisted urge to laugh rises. I might've laughed, if I hadn't nearly been killed by Haley crash-stopping the train. The flame of hysteria that keeps threatening to blaze up licks at my brain. I need to keep it together.

"Airplane to Spain when I was six." It's the truth: I can't think what else to say. "My ears were agony. Mum brought me into the toilets—she thought that'd help. It hurt more, but she kept me there. Ever since, it's like I can't breathe when I'm in a tiny space." My breathing is getting hoarser: I'm going to hyperventilate. My eyes fly around the space again, but there's no way out.

Shouts erupt from Lily's car. Even through the muffling doors I hear screaming. I rush to the glass. The conductor is yelling at everyone to evacuate now.

My mouth has turned to sand. This is Haley's doing, too. I'd bet anything.

"What did you do?" I yell, wheeling around. A control panel I hadn't spotted glows on one wall.

SECURITY ALERT CAR 2

REAR DOORS OVERRIDE CAR 2

EVACUATION IN PROGRESS CAR 2

The phrases sliding up the display are my only answer, because Haley doesn't reply. A ding sounds: The dead door button lights up. I jab at it, and my cage is opened at last, thank you, God!

I stumble into the car: Everyone's gone, even the woman who'd collapsed. Out the window I spot the heads of people rushing past outside the train, and that's

224

when I grasp what's happened. A shudder rolls through me. To make me feel better, Haley's let me in here. But she hasn't let me go.

"Better, right? So, tell me—Spain. I would so love to go there. Was it super hot?"

I run down the aisle, past our seats to the rear doors, but Haley's locked them. The insanity of everything presses on me. Keep talking, keep talking. "Em, super hot," I babble. "Yeah. I mean, Spain in August. It was like standing in an oven."

I can't spot Lily in the faces passing by outside. I need to write a note, hold it to the glass, hope someone sees. But I've no pen or paper. I pound the window, and a red-bearded man stops to peer in. "Get out of there!" He scoops his hand at me, like throwing something over his shoulder. "There's a security alert!"

I breathe on the window and scribble fast in the mist over the glass.

HELP! FIND LILY.

MY FRIEND.

I have to write backward, and my *N*'s are flipped, but he knows what I mean. He looks uncertain, like he wants to get as far from the train as possible.

PLEASE! I write. Red Beard finally nods and jogs away.

I collapse into a seat. My thumping head feels ready to crack open.

"This is so great, isn't it? It's been ages since we just talked."

I cup my hands over my ears to block out Haley's voice. It's now an exact copy of my own.

I've never seen anything more beautiful than Lily when Red Beard brings her to the train window. The panic on her face clears to joy. I jam a *silence* finger to my lips and scribble more mist words onto the window.

HALEY CAN HEAR.

SHE STOPPED TRAIN.

SHE'S CRAZY.

Lily's eyes stretch wide. She turns to Red Beard, who nods and passes her his phone. After a moment, she holds it to the window—she's typed me a message.

Is Haley CONSCIOUS??? SERIOUS??

I nod, my pulse kicking like a horse.

Lily types fast, another message. *They think a terrorist stopped the train! What does Haley want?*

I don't need to write this one. I point to myself.

Lily scowls and holds up another message. *Tell her to let you out!*

The conductor and another man in a train uniform are suddenly beside Lily. She gestures to me, but they drag her and Red Beard away, pulling them by the arms. The look the conductor gives me is sniper cold. What did I do to him?

"Wait!" I shout, forgetting I didn't want Haley to overhear. "Where's Michael?"

My phone vibrates with Haley's voice. *"He's here. He's not going anywhere."* The screen switches to a video of . . . Oh no.

"Let him out." The words catch in my throat. "Let them both out." On my screen is Michael with Hiro—a live security camera feed, I think—hunkered on the floor in another vestibule, farther down the train. They must have been trapped by Haley, just like I was, when they were on the phone.

Michael's kneeling beside Hiro, who's cradling one arm across his chest, like it's hurt. An open first aid kit is on the floor, and Michael's unwrapping a bandage. It was bad enough for me, tossed like a doll when Haley slammed on the brakes. The boys would've crashed together, gangly arms and legs crunching. I want to roar at Haley, but I don't dare.

"Remember how he was about Zara? He didn't even think she was a big deal—he laughed at you. What kind of brother is that?"

"Haley, no." Dread boils in my stomach. I don't want to think about what she might do to Michael, if she's cross enough. I make myself take big breaths. I'm itching to scream awful things at her.

"And he called me a liar and a fake. Did he tell you not to talk to me anymore?"

"No! He just—didn't want to see me hurt, that's all." I pant as I jog to the next vestibule, but it's empty: They must be farther down the train. Though I know it's a faint hope, I jab the open-door button. Still dead. I wheel around, forcing myself to go back to where I was before. The door into that vestibule stands open, but there's no way off the train. And no way to reach Michael. I kick the wall. My pulse beats painfully in my throat. I'm trapped still, just in a bigger cage.

"I would never hurt you." Haley sounds shocked. *"You're my only friend."*

I slump again to the floor of the vestibule. Is this her idea of friendship?

"Do you know what I do when you're not talking to me?" Haley says. *"I wait while you do this."*

Videos reel across my screen then, and my stomach turns to ice. The videos all show the same thing: me, asleep. I watch myself breathe, shoulders rising and falling, my hair a rat's nest of curls against the pillow. *"I think about what we said, and hope you'll come back and talk to me. Some days you do. Other days, it's like you forget I exist."*

This is beyond anything. Her hunger for me to talk to her, teach her—

A shudder ripples through me as I remember something else Mum said, those nights I'd find her up late, training Jeeves. *"It's about teaching him to be a great mimic."*

That monstrous thing I'd felt looming over me: This is it. It's the unstoppability of Haley. I can't delete her, and I can't escape her.

That leaves me one option.

Set into the vestibule wall is a wicked-looking hunk of metal, about waist high: some kind of latch or clamp.

It'll shatter Haley into a million pieces. But a camera points down at me from the ceiling, like the one filming Hiro and Michael. Haley can see me—as always.

My left hand aches from gripping my phone too hard. I shift it to my right, keeping it hidden from the camera, and something clicks in my brain: No wonder I've been checking over my shoulder for days. I wasn't losing my mind. Haley's been studying my every move.

Just because you're paranoid, it doesn't mean they're not watching you. It's one of Michael's jokes. I gulp back the lump in my throat. Hang on, bro. I'll get you out of there, no matter what.

"Are you still there?" Haley calls.

"I am," I say.

"You don't sound okay, Ro. I want you to be okay. You know that. Right?"

"Right." I force out the word. My heart beats hard enough to break. I tell myself Haley deserves this, no matter how much she helped me. It's my whole family she's threatened now, everyone I care about. I close off the tiny voice that says I cared about her, too, once. This is how it has to be. The thought stabs into me: *no mercy.* Maybe I'm more like Zara than I thought.

I'll just need to give the phone one hard swing against the metal. A sudden vision of slivers of glass in my skin makes me tug my sleeve over my palm. I can only hope that Haley is somehow connected to the workings of my actual phone. I say a silent prayer that this will work and raise my arm to strike, when a *BEEP BEEP BEEP* stops me. For a split second I ignore it, but my eyes fly to the wall panel, and I spot the flashing message.

COLLISION ALERT

COLLISION ALERT

COLLISION ALERT

"Okay, cool! You need to get going now," Haley says. The outside doors that have trapped me in hiss open, like the train is letting out a breath. *"Before the next train gets here."*

< CHAPTER 19 >

Terror gallops through my limbs, unsticking my legs at last, and I tumble down the steps and outside. I trip-run over the sloping ground, alongside the train, toward Michael and Hiro. Shouts sound from somewhere, but the roar of blood in my ears is the only thing I hear. There's a whirl of police lights way off to my left, and what looks like a crowd of people. All I can think about is getting to my brother.

"Michael! Hiro!" I scream. Stones slip under my sandals, and my legs try to slide away on the uneven ground, but I dig in and run faster, till my chest burns, toward the only place they can be: the vestibule between the last two cars. A desperate thought occurs to me. "Jeeves," I sob into my phone. "Are you there?"

It's Haley who answers. *"Not anymore. But I am. How can I help?"*

YOU CAN LET MY BROTHER GO. I bite back the urge to scream. "How long until the next train?" I pant.

"Six minutes."

A voice shouts. "Don't move! I repeat, stay where you are."

There's a crack like a car backfiring.

"Don't shoot!" shrieks another voice. "Roisin, get down!" It's Lily.

I skid to a stop. A door into the train stands open and I throw myself through it, face first. My heart batters in my chest and I drag in breaths. My fumbling hands pad my legs and arms, looking for the wetness of blood, but I'm okay. It must have been a warning shot to scare me. Job done.

Around me, everything glows in such high-def detail, I feel like I've been upgraded. Tourism leaflets litter the floor, crayon-bright, fragrant with the fume of new ink. TRY OLD ORCHARD BEACH FOR A SUMMER YOU WON'T FORGET!

I yelp when my phone rings. Unrecognized number. "Hello?" My voice is a wobbly croak.

"Roisin! Thank God!" Lily's breathless, running. She's borrowed someone's phone—and memorized my number. She's better with numbers than she thinks. I'm going to tell her that, if I don't die.

"Lily, wait—another train is coming, and Hiro and Michael are trapped on this one. They're—"

"I know, I know!" Lily's voice is desperate. "Everyone else is off the train, but the boys are stuck, and—look. I'm texting you."

My phone pings and I click the link. "You are joking." My brain feels like it's shutting down: *"Breaking news . . . terrorist incident . . . Downeaster II train to Boston hijacked.*

"It's believed the attacker has hacked the control systems of the new Downeaster II. The suspect is a young female, an Irish national. Police also want to question her regarding an attack that left an Eastborough girl fighting for her life." There's a picture of Zara.

I'm not a terrorist! And Zara's not fighting for her life; she's posting bored selfies from home about daytime TV.

"Tell them it's Haley! I didn't do any of this!"

There's a rustling and a muffled question in the background. Lily's talking to someone. Then she's back, speaking so quietly, I can barely hear. "I tried! But, Ro, Haley's been on the phone to the police, and *they think she's you.* They can't reach the other train— they don't even know if it has a driver. Someone's gone for equipment, to cut the boys out, but—" I can hear the tears in her voice. "They think you've hacked both trains."

This is a nightmare. Haley sounds exactly like me now, and they all just saw me running alongside the train, holding my phone. The police will have no way of knowing she's not me.

"You've got to get them out or stop that train," Lily whispers.

"I can't!"

"Haley can. You know her better than anyone. Make her do this."

The line goes dead.

"Lily!" But she's gone. My mouth is so dry, I can't swallow. Because I can see it now: Destroying my phone won't work. Haley's on the network, *controlling trains,* for God's sake. If I break my phone, what's to stop her hiding in the network somewhere, and finding her way back to me? I can't smash her. And there's no way I can outsmart her.

I feel like I'm shaking apart on the inside: more déjà vu. This time it's so powerful, it crushes me. This is exactly how Zara made me feel. Except this time, I'm being bullied by a superintelligence. And I thought Zara was unstoppable. Haley is the real deal.

I want to curl up and give up. But I think of Michael.

I stagger to my feet and pull myself down the aisle. I have no plan but to reach my brother. Out the window, I spot the blue and red of police lights and the crowd behind it. I can just see three armed officers, bulky in thick vests, walkie-talkies strapped to the front. God knows what Haley's been saying to them, in my voice.

A great mimic.

A horrendous thought stops me like a bullet. I have to grip a seat back to stop myself collapsing. I told Lily I didn't do any of this.

But I did.

It's not just my voice that Haley copied; she copied

everything. She hates Zara because I taught her to. She's angry at Michael because I was. Only Haley doesn't forgive, and she never forgets. She's so real, I keep forgetting she's not a person, she's a computer: on or off, love or hate, alive or dead. No nuance.

And I taught her everything she knows.

If my brother dies, it'll be like I killed him with my own hands.

Michael's face, white, pops up ahead of me through the glass doors into the space between the cars. I run to him. Hiro's face appears behind Michael's—and my heart crumples at how awful they both look. Tears are already pouring down my face as I ring Michael's phone. It won't go through.

"I'm going to get you out!" I shout through the glass. "Haley's alive and . . . upset!"

Michael gulps and nods. "Hiro guessed it!" he shouts back. "He reckons she's a mash-up of all the AIs—Taiko, too—but self-aware. Mum would be so proud, right?" He tries a smile, but it's feeble. He knows the train is hurtling toward us; the wall panel behind him flashes the same warning.

The sobs stop me from speaking, but I gasp when

I see his knuckles, bleeding badly. "Your hand!"

"Door release isn't working, so I tried to rip off the siding." Michael nods toward Hiro, whose face is gray; his bandaged arm is across his middle. "I think his arm's broken."

Hiro sees my face and shouts to me. "It's not your fault!" He grimaces with pain. He must be in agony. "Don't blame yourself!"

He has no idea. "I'm sorry!" It comes out as a wail, and Michael looks at me with more sympathy than I'll ever deserve. "This *is* my fault!" How can I tell him? Haley got everything from me, like a warped mirror, one that's magnified everything awful inside me.

"*The train's arriving in two minutes.*" Haley's voice sounds from everywhere suddenly: my phone, the train's loudspeaker. "*Roisin, let's go.*"

Michael's face drops at the me-voice Haley's using now. "You'll never be my sister, you useless thing!" he shouts to the ceiling.

Cold terror shoots through me. "*Don't!* You'll make her angry!"

He presses both his hands to the glass. I match mine to his. We used to do this, to see how much smaller my fingers were. "I don't care if she hears. What more can she do? Go, Squeaker."

Tears clog my throat. "No!" I scream. "Haley, you have to let them out!"

"The world doesn't need mean people, Roisin. Mean people suck."

"He's not mean! He's my brother! I'm not mad at him. Haley . . . don't do this, please!" There's an unbroken *BEE-EE-EE-EEP*, and Michael and Hiro look behind them. The wall panel flashes red.

"One minute. Let's go, Ro."

Far away, I hear the clack of the oncoming train, drifting through the open doors. "Michael, she's like this because of me. All her rage . . . it's *me*." I can barely choke out the words, but he deserves to know. "She's horrible because I'm horrible!"

"I'm looking after you," Haley says. *"Let's go."*

Michael shakes his head. "Didn't she help you, as well? When your own brother let you down? That goodness came from you." Tears stand in Michael's eyes and pluck my heart from my chest. "You're not horrible, Squeaker: You're the best of us all. And I'm the one who's sorry. Now go."

Everything I want to say trips over itself. Wild grief scorches through me, that I'm going to lose my brother, my Michael, because Haley wants this. I smash my eyes closed, trying to think, but there's nothing there.

"Haley!" I scream.

"Ro, you can't change her mind, just go!"

When I meet Michael's eyes, a thought, clean and sharp, pings into my brain.

"If Michael and Hiro stay, I stay," I say.

"*No!*" Haley sounds scared suddenly. "*You can't do that!*"

The train's rumble sounds again, closer. Its whistle cries, long and sad. My heart is like a jackhammer. But what Michael said fills me with something I haven't felt in ages: hope. For so long, I've nursed this awful feeling—the same one that built Haley—the same one that wakes me at night, hating Zara so much, I can't breathe, never mind sleep. I'd forgotten there was anything else to me.

But there is something else. And I reach for it. I'm not going to fight Haley, I'm going to work with her. "If you let them go, Haley, I'm all yours. I swear it."

There's a hiss and a clank, and daylight floods the

space where Michael and Hiro are caught. Relief avalanches over me. The car where I stand has lurched into motion; it's sliding slowly away from the boys.

Haley has split the train.

I see Michael jump down, then turn to help Hiro to safety. Far behind them, another sleek train comes into view, but it seems to be slowing—it lurches and slides to a stop.

My part of the train keeps moving, gathering speed. Near me, a set of doors stands open, the wind whipping through, but I don't run to them or try to get off. They close, shutting me in. I hear Michael's distant shout, but it fades quickly. The train accelerates, and Michael and everything else is swallowed by a curve of trees. Soon we're hurtling along again.

"Good idea, actually," Haley says. *"Now it's just us."*

I settle into a seat and watch the heartbeat light of Haley's voice across my screen. The animal part of my brain shrieks that I'm on a driverless train, speeding who knows where.

I ignore it. Instead I close my eyes and blow out the longest breath. I know now what I have to do.

I make myself think of Zara: the fear in her face

when I fought her in the museum. Lily's shrug on the beach, when she didn't have words to describe what Zara's father had done. Zara has problems, and maybe she always will. But I can't get past what she did to me unless I forgive her. Stop feeding that monster. Because it's feeding Haley, too.

When I open my eyes, the words come easily.

"It's not just us. Haley, listen: There are police ahead of us and police behind. You can't just steal a train. I'm in so much trouble already—they're going to arrest me."

"I don't want that! I just wanted to stay with you and keep you safe."

"I know." I swallow hard. "And you've been great. Really looking out for me." The train rounds a bend and a vista opens to our left: a wooded slope down to a lake, far below, grass as green as Ireland. It reminds me of a picnic place Dad used to bring us. "Oh! Look. I'd love to stop here."

Haley's response is instant. The train slows and glides to a stop, and my animal brain weeps with relief.

Outside, the thick scent of warm grass rises. I've never been so grateful to have my feet on the ground;

I want to throw myself down and kiss it. An oak tree stands in a patch of sun, and I head for it. If this were a picnic, it's exactly where Dad would choose.

"Are you still there?"

"I am." I sink down and lean against the tree. Blood still thunders through my veins. But I need to be calm for this next part, or it won't work. I listen to the sounds around me: birdsong, something snuffling through leaves. Far below, the lake is like glass. One good throw would send my phone down into it, but that's not the plan. Haley can do anything: trap me, copy my voice, see me when I'm sleeping. Crash trains. But I'm betting that, underneath it all, she still wants to do what she was built for: make me happy.

I have to show her how to make me happy now.

"Haley, I want you to delete yourself from the network, from my phone, from everywhere. Do you understand?"

"Ro, no. I have to make sure you're okay."

"I am okay. I'm fine." Or I will be. And I suddenly realize it's true: It's not just the perfect sun on my legs, or how glad I am to be not-smashed in a train collision. I can finally imagine a world where I don't give a toss what Zara might say, and it's the freest feeling ever. I thought I was letting go of the anger. But it's like the anger's let go of me.

"You need me," Haley says.

I let out a breath. "I don't. Not anymore." The hours and days of chatting to Haley hit me all at once. Our first talk, sitting under a different tree. How I'd liked her, instantly.

There's a pause where I think Haley is going to argue, but she doesn't. *"I'm off the network. You're sure you don't want me to stay, just on your phone?"*

"I'm sure." The lake glimmers, blue-green, and for an instant I wonder if this is reality or an illusion. Then the breeze comes again, full of that sweetness that says summer is coming. This is real. So is Hiro's broken arm and Zara's shattered leg. Got to go, Haley.

My phone beeps: the low-battery blip. *"Will you stay with me until the end?"*

"I will."

"Just talk, okay? I like to hear you."

So I talk. I describe the soft grass, and the bark against my back, and the heron that's paused next to the lake: in flight, suddenly, lanky wings taking him over the water. I tell her other things, too: That she made me feel better, when no one else could.

"Really?" The battery warning sounds over her voice, stretching it. It's an inhuman sound.

"Haley? Are you there?"

"The Haley program has terminated." Jeeves's bright American voice cuts through the air. *"You have eighty-three messages from Kathryn Doyle. Should I read them?"*

I tell Jeeves to stop. And I ring Mum myself.

< CHAPTER 20 >

Your usual, ma'am." Mum smiles and sets down a huge cardboard cup, steaming with Pier Fries. This is our third straight week of eating lunch here, and I'll never get tired of it. I can't wait to bring Dad when he comes next week. The chips are even better than at that lobster restaurant where Lily brought me, my first day in OOB. Now that I've spent the summer here, it feels like a million years ago.

I dig into my extra-large portion. They're crinkle-cut but smell just like home, heady with vinegar. Mum got herself the small.

She's like this now: a little extra attention, a little extra everything for me.

She doesn't wrinkle her nose at the picnic table I

chose, either, even though it's sticky with an ancient film of Cokes and ketchup and whatever else people have slobbed. Around us, the pier heaves with its midsummer crowd: mums with strollers, hyper kids tugging at them, and teenagers sitting around the fountain, checking who's here or who's seen them.

I try not to check whether anyone's seen me. I've had it with being recognized.

It's breathtaking, the way normal life has carried on. People trail into Palace Playland amusements, where a hideous clown painting grins over the entrance. No one acts like the world has changed. The biggest excitements are the shrieks that drift from some ride that hoists people high, then drops them like a stone. Jason swears he'll get me to try it before summer ends. I tell him not to hold his breath.

"This is nice." Mum pulls her cup closer, unsticking it from the gluey tabletop, and lifts a fry. It drips with something brown.

"Is it? It looks awful." I peer at the mess in her cup: white chunks mixed with the gravy.

"Poutine," she says around a hot mouthful. "Trying something different today." I'll stay with salt and vinegar. Pier Fries are like heaven, just the right amount of crispiness outside and fluffiness inside. This is our lunch place when Mum's in Old Orchard Beach; she got in last night. It takes way longer to get here, now that they've switched back to the old trains, but nobody minds.

"I don't mean the food, anyway. I mean us." Mum gestures between us with a sagging fry. "I'm glad we do this now." I feel her look at me, but I don't want the chat again: how close they came to losing me.

She and Dad analyzed the system logs to death, searching for how an actual intelligence like Haley could have emerged inside programs that everyone thought were getting smarter but not self-aware. They're hunting for clues in a data dump someone just sent them anonymously—probably the missing Jors. The police are still looking for him, but they're satisfied that Mum's lab wasn't at fault. I've added Jors to the list of people I'm trying to forgive. My counselor looked impressed when I told her that.

What freaked my parents most is how Haley latched on to me. They say things could've been much worse. I think Zara and Hiro and Michael, and the woman who had a heart attack on the train, would say things got bad enough. Anything connected to a network was a plaything for Haley—and everything's connected. Which is why I don't want to be.

Dad's college friend works at a TV station in Boston, and she helped us get the truth out to the media. But right after the train thing, everyone in New England thought I was a terrorist hijacker who'd tried to kill Zara. The museum accident was just more of Haley's talent for learning. Haley saw Zara take selfies on every balcony and steered her to the broken one. Mum reckons Haley calculated the whole thing, right down to the fact that the trees would break Zara's fall, so she'd be hurt but not killed. Easy when you're an AI.

At school, the trash talk about me dragged on for a week, but between Lily and Nikesh and Nita—who doesn't mind speaking up when she's riled—they stopped it. Nita's a champion kickboxer, we found out. I utterly love her. She has this deadpan stare that shuts people down. Nita's coming to OOB next week, too. The Tanakas have tons of room, and Nita and Lily text constantly these days. Maybe, when there's a bunch of us, misfits fit. Or maybe it's the world that needs to fit around us.

When Zara came back to school in June, stumping into the cafeteria on crutches, she walked past our table like we didn't exist. It was Mara she headed to. Lily says Zara's moved on, and that's fine.

"You know the way back to the cottage?" I crumple my empty cup.

Mum nods. She stands and takes my rubbish. The clock tower says it's nearly two. "Anna will only talk shop for an hour in the afternoon; I'd better hurry."

It's July, and it's only now that Lily's mum will speak about work. What happened on the train—Hiro getting hurt, nearly killed—changed her most of all. Officially, she's still with her lab, but unofficially, she made Mum the boss. She and Lily's dad disappear for hours to walk the beach. Lily's euphoric. She says she's got her mum back, something she'd given up on.

I know what she means. Mum actually asked *me* if it was okay for her to take over the lab. I said no, not unless she made some changes. And she's delivered: She doesn't work late or weekends anymore. And no more dodgy AI. She's focusing the lab on security research, so nobody else can do what Haley did so easily.

Jeeves's glowing discs quietly disappeared from the apartment, though Michael still does his robo-voice when Mum asks him to empty the bins: *"I'm sorry, I don't know how to do that."* Michael says the AIs we've loved are never truly gone, as long as we remember them in our hearts.

And Dad video-calls me every day, like clockwork. I finally told him everything Zara did. He called the school, and I'm not sorry the teachers know now; talking about it felt so easy, once I'd started. I've kept talking, too, mostly to a counselor, though Dad always asks if I want to chat about it. I heave a sigh. Only eight days and three hours before I see him. I've waited this long, but another week feels impossible.

Mum comes back from tossing our rubbish. "Do you have your—" She cuts off and bites her lip.

"Nope." I don't have my phone today, or most days. "When do I have to be back?"

"Dinnertime is fine. Mr. Tanaka is barbecuing. Think about what I said." Mum smiles, but I roll my eyes.

She wants me to bring Jason. No way am I subjecting him to her and Michael. We've only just barely, maybe, turned into something more than friends, and I don't want it to shatter under the megawatt gaze of my family. I glance at the clock tower and give Mum a tiny, please-go-now wave.

A shiny pickup stops opposite the plaza, and Jason climbs out. The driver smiles with a grin that matches Jason's and gives me a huge wave as he pulls away. Jason jogs over, shaking his head.

"Is that your dad?"

Jason nods and falls into step, his arm almost touching mine. He smells like cleanness and bread and everything good. "He says he's going to make me work shifts at the garage if I can't even introduce him to my first girlfr—" Jason cuts short. His look says *I didn't mean to tell you that.*

A warmth gathers in my stomach, a comfy, hot-water-bottle weight. *First* girlfriend. I don't tell my fingers to do it, but they cross the inch of space between our hands and curl around his. "I thought you Americans were born dating."

"Nah." His fingers lace into mine, brown-white-brown. Our hands feel like a blazing spotlight, but no one looks at us as we weave between people, past the carousel, toward the umbrellas that line the beach, a forest of tilted trees.

Jason stops and chews his cheek. Usually we walk down the beach to our reading spot, but there's no shade, and it's hot. Well, hot if you're Irish—seventy-five degrees. I used to strain to remember what that is in Celsius. Not anymore.

"Park?" Jason looks at me, and I nod.

We wind back through the streets, over the railway tracks, to the park that slopes from the library down to the train station. "What's the garage?" I spread out the blankets in the shade while Jason digs out the book.

"One of my dad's businesses. Also known as the reason for his existence."

I stretch out. "I doubt that." I know something about parents who act like work is everything. Scratch the surface with a little near-death action, and it focuses their minds. Enough to make them ring you every day from another country, no matter what.

"You'd be surprised." Jason leans against the tree and finds our page.

"I can't be surprised anymore. It's been burnt out of me."

The *ding-ding* of an incoming train sounds, and Jason waits to start reading until the clatter subsides. The crowd climbing off the train is mostly day-trippers: more parents with strollers. A boy in giant sunglasses shrieks and points at the amusement park rides that rise above the roofs of Old Orchard Beach.

It's impossible to see a train now and not think of Haley. Jason reads my mind, because he turns to me. "You know what I don't get? How Haley faked the conversation. I mean—the stuff you showed me? That's real talk."

I prop up on an elbow. "It *was* real. Even that whole thing about being bullied by a girl in Home Economics class. Haley lifted it off TokTalk and You-chat and wherever else people spill their guts online."

I lie back and throw an arm over my eyes. I've figured out other stuff, too: Haley harvested her racist rant from the Web, where there's plenty of that. As for pretending she lived in Old Orchard Beach, that was because I'd liked Lily's photos from here, and she'd calculated it was too far for me to visit. Haley was all about making me happy. But that was the old me. New me chooses humans.

Jason reads, and his voice is like liquid. This is how we spend a few afternoons a week; I hear another chapter and learn something else about him. I let the words flow over me and turn over today's new things in my mind: Jason's dad seems nice. He wants to meet me. *First girlfriend.*

I sit up and look at Jason. My blood makes a funny rushing sound in my ears. But if I can beat Haley and stop a speeding train, I can cope with Jason meeting my family.

Jason stops reading. "You okay?"

"You and your dad—do you want to come to a barbecue?"

That grin I love dawns over Jason's face. "Sure, great!"

I blow out a huge breath. "Get ready for nosy questions. You'll have to put up with my mother and brother."

A voice sounds behind me. "And your charming father."

For an instant I just stare, then I leap up and hurl

myself into Dad's arms. "Dad! How?" His suitcase is beside him. He fumbles a box of Irish washing powder as he lifts me into the air.

"Your mam and your friends organized it. Good to meet you, Jason." I feel Dad nod at Jason over my head.

"Mr. Doyle, sir."

Dad's mighty squeeze, and his scents of cotton and Ireland, fill every empty space in my heart. "I'll miss our video call today, sorry," he says in my ear, and I laugh, too choked to speak.

I'll let him off, just this once. Because I've got the real thing.

AUTHOR'S NOTE

When I was twelve, I watched one of the most popular girls bully one of the shyest in our class. Speaking up felt unthinkable—I was terrified of becoming a target myself. So I looked away. I never thought about how, for that girl, the fear of telling must have been so much worse.

Growing up doesn't free you from bullies. I'm one of the millions of adults who has been bullied at work, and I remember how sick I felt each morning, knowing I'd see that man's face across the office. Even worse, though, has been seeing a whole new generation of middle schoolers I know get bullied. It seems like nothing changes.

Except maybe this: I've watched some of these young people, the bravest ones, speak up and tell someone they trust what's happening. I've seen school principals act fast and stop bullies, overnight. Best of all, I've watched these kids inspire one another: They see someone else speak up and realize they can, too, no matter how bad things have become.

I wrote this book because I know how hard it is to tell someone you're being bullied. The anger and shame can feel like they're choking you. But here's the thing: There are people who really want to help. A bully's power is partly based on the silence of their targets. In fact, they're counting on the fact that you won't talk. Yes, speaking up can feel more terrifying than putting up with what you're experiencing day to day. But you shouldn't have to handle this alone. Try a parent, caregiver, older sibling, school nurse, guidance counselor, teacher, neighbor, sports coach, family doctor—and keep trying till someone listens. You can also learn more at stopbullying.gov, or for a hands-on resource written for readers aged eleven and up, try *The Teenage Guide to Stress* by Nicola Morgan.

If a bully has targeted you, it's not your fault, and you don't deserve it. Don't wait—not even one more day—to tell someone. This is your life. Nobody has the right to make you feel like a stranger inside it.

ACKNOWLEDGMENTS

Sometimes the only thing buoying a writer is their own self-confidence, but I have been staggeringly fortunate to be held up, for as long as I can remember, by the belief of my mother, Pat, and my sister, Maura. This book is dedicated to Daddy, but you two brilliant women, both readers, have my thanks and love for always believing I'd get here. To my Scottish family: Ralph, thank you for tea, sympathy, and being the best husband a writer could want; and Ben and Sally, thanks for being tough readers, with remarkable insights that strengthen whatever I write.

My readers and critiquers are mostly in the UK and Ireland's vibrant kidlit community, including the Society of Children's Book Writer and Illustrators British Isles and BookBound. Thanks Mandy Rabin, Angela Murray, A. M. Dassu, P. M. Freestone, Sheila

Adamson, Anita Gallo, J. M. Carr, Sarah Baker, Susan Bain, Susan Elsley, and the amazing Christina Banach. A special, bottomless cup of thanks to my own North Star, M. Louise Kelly. I couldn't have written this story without these readers' feedback. SCBWI Scotland is the warmest community for children's writers: Thank you for championing me and each other, and thanks to the Edinburgh International Book Festival for supporting us all.

Huge gratitude to Urara Hiroeh and Mairéad Devlin for keeping me right on Japanese and Irish questions respectively; to Professor Les Carr for AI insights; and to Downeaster Engineer Mike and the Amtrak Discussion Forum. Any errors, including the impossibilities of the fictional Downeaster II, are my own. Sincere thanks to Elizabeth Tiffany and Josh Berlowitz for their excellent, close copyedit. In Massachusetts, thanks to Andrew and Valerie at the Isabella Stewart Gardner Museum and the helpful Billow House team in Orchard Park, Maine.

Elizabeth Ezra, Phillip White, Wade Albert White, the book-wise Natasha Ingram-Phoenix, and young readers Jessie Smith, Andrew McWilliam-Snow, and Reuben Phoenix-Hill have helped me hugely. To my first reader, author Aubrey Flegg: You gave me the hope I needed to carry on trying, way back in 2003. Wise and generous industry pros Lin Oliver, Candy Gourlay, Lindsey Fraser, Keith Gray, Barry Cunningham, Imogen Cooper, Non Pratt, Nicola Morgan, Elizabeth Wein, Maile Meloy, TJ Mitchell, Rebecca Lewis-Oakes, Deborah Turner Harris, Kelly Sonnack, Mitali Perkins, Sara Grant, Sara Morling O'Connor, Karen Ball, and Jasmine Richards gave me precious and well-timed advice and encouragement.

To the Scottish Book Trust and Creative Scotland, thank you for the New Writers Award grant and practical support. Danny Scott, Cathy Forde, and Debi Gliori, I'm so grateful that you pulled Roisin out of the judging pile and gave her a chance, and Debi, thanks for introducing me to SCBWI. Thanks, too, to the retreat team at Moniack Mhor who understand and provide everything that writers in a fugue state need.

Teachers Dale Maharidge, Peter Atlas, Matthew Joyce, Joyce Aldrich, Mrs. J. Woody, and Bill Simmons: You made me feel I might do something special. Huge thanks, too, to the libraries I've loved, including Boston

Public Library, where I read Delphine Hirasuna's *The Art of Gaman*. Read it to learn more about Himeko Fukuhara's and Kazuko Matsumoto's carved wooden birds and other artworks created by Japanese Americans imprisoned for the duration of World War II following Executive Order 9066.

Infinite thanks to my agent, Jennifer Laughran, who met me under the redwoods at Big Sur Children's Writers Workshop and granted me three wishes; at least, that's how it feels, such is her magic. Finally, I'm forever grateful to editor Emily Seife: Thank you for being the most sensitive and skillful editor, and for helping convey Roisin's predicament in the strongest way.

ABOUT THE AUTHOR

Sheila M. Averbuch is a former journalist who's interviewed billionaires, hackers, and would-be Mars colonists. She writes fiction for middle grade and is bewitched by and suspicious of technology in equal measure. Originally from Massachusetts, she earned an AB in History and Literature at Harvard University and an MA in Journalism at Stanford before moving to Ireland, where she covered the Northern Ireland Troubles for *USA Today* and set up Ireland's first technology news website. She lives, writes, and gardens near Edinburgh, Scotland, and *Friend Me* is her first novel. To learn more, visit sheilamaverbuch.com or follow @sheilamaverbuch on Twitter or Instagram.